ILLUSTRATED CLASSICS

The Adventures
of
Tom Sawyer

by
Mark Twain

Adapted by
Bookmatrix Ltd

Edited by
Claire Black

Published by

Berryland
Books
www.berrylandbooks.com

The Adventures of Tom Sawyer

by

Mark Twain

First Published in 2006 • Copyright © Berryland Books 2006
ISBN 1-84577-594-5 • Printed in India

Contents

CHAPTER I

Meeting Tom Sawyer

Tom Sawyer had landed himself in trouble, yet again.

First he had been caught eating forbidden jam in the morning, and then, in the afternoon, he had played hooky from school and Aunt Polly had come to know of it.

Not that it was the first time all these accidents

had happened to Tom, who lived with his aunt, Cousin Mary and younger half-brother Sid. He was always getting into some sort of trouble or other, and as a result was constantly driving his poor Aunt Polly mad. She forever hovered in between annoyance and concern whether she was doing her duty by her dead sister's child.

"Every time I let him off, my conscience does hurt me so, and every time I hit him, my old heart almost breaks!"

However, that day Aunt Polly had made up her mind on punishing Tom for his mischief. During supper that night, she tried to trap him into revealing that he skipped school. The cunning Tom had almost succeeded in averting Aunt Polly's questioning, until Sid played spoilsport and squelched on him.

While Tom swore bashing up Sid for telling on him, Aunt Polly decided to snatch away Tom's Saturday freedom as punishment.

Next afternoon, Tom got into a scuffle with a

bully downtown. When finally he returned home late at night, and climbed in at the window, he was met head-on by none other than Aunt Polly! And when she glanced at his torn and dirty clothes, her resolution to punish him became firmer and she sentenced him to painting the entire fence during his Saturday holiday.

So, on the bright and fresh Saturday morning, Tom appeared on the sidewalk with a bucket of whitewash and a long-handled brush. He inspected the nine feet high, thirty yards long fence, and sighed deeply. As he thought of the fun he had planned for this day, the sorrows of the poor boy multiplied. Soon his friends would come tripping along and make fun of him for having to work; and this very thought burnt Tom's heart like fire.

It was at this dark and hopeless moment that an inspiration burst upon him. Nothing less than a great, magnificent inspiration!

Tom took up his brush and calmly began his

work. Soon, Ben Rogers, the boy whose ridicule Tom had been dreading the most, came in sight, eating an apple. Tom went on whitewashing, paying no attention to Ben. As Ben drew near Tom, he slackened his speed and stared at the boy, seemingly hard at work.

Although Tom's mouth watered for the juicy-looking apple in Ben's hand, he stuck to his work.

"Hello, old chap, you got to work, hey?" cried Ben. "Say, I'm going swimming. Don't you want to go too? But of course you have to work!"

"Well, it may be work, or maybe not," Tom answered carelessly. "All I know is it suits Tom Sawyer."

"Oh come now, you don't mean to say that you like whitewashing?" said Ben, disbelievingly.

"Well, I don't see why I should not like it!" declared Tom. "Does a boy get a chance to whitewash a fence every day?"

Tom's argument put the thing in an entirely

new light and Ben stopped nibbling his apple. As he watched attentively, Tom elegantly swept his brush back and forth, stepped back to note the effect, and added a touch here and there. Ben observed Tom's every move and got more and more interested, more and more absorbed.

At last he said, "Say, Tom, let me do the whitewashing for some time."

Although Tom was dying to do exactly that, he declared shrewdly, "No, no, Aunt Polly is very particular about this fence; it's got to be whitewashed very carefully. I think there isn't one boy in a thousand, maybe two thousand, who can do it correctly."

"Oh, shucks, I'll be just as careful. Let me do it for a while," pleaded Ben. "See, I'll give you this apple."

With a greatly reluctant face, Tom gave up his brush to Ben. And while the victorious Ben worked and sweated in the sun, Tom sat on a barrel in the shade close by, dangled his legs, and munched his apple.

There was no lack of helping hands. Boys came along every little while; they came to laugh, but remained to whitewash. By the time Ben was tired out, Tom had traded the next chance to Billy Fisher for a kite; and when Billy was exhausted, Johnny Miller bought his place for a dead rat and a string to swing it with; and so on, and so on, and hour after hour.

And when the middle of the afternoon came, from being a poor poverty-stricken boy in the morning, Tom was literally rolling in wealth. He had to do absolutely nothing all morning—he had plenty of company—and the fence had three coats of whitewash on it!

If he hadn't run out of paint, Tom would have bankrupted every boy in the village.

When Tom approached Aunt Polly, she was nodding over her knitting and her cat was asleep in her lap. Her spectacles were propped up on her gray head for safety. Aunt Polly had been sure that as usual, Tom must have run away long ago. But now, seeing him place himself in her power again in this intrepid way, she was taken by surprise.

"May I go and play now, aunt?" asked Tom.

"What, already? How much have you done?"

"It's all done, aunt."

Aunt Polly had little faith in her nephew's words and went out to see for herself. But when she found the entire fence whitewashed—and not only whitewashed but elaborately coated and recoated—her astonishment was almost unspeakable.

"Well, I never!" she exclaimed. "You can work when you've a mind to, Tom."

"Well, go along and play," she told him, quite pleased inwardly, "but mind you, get back in time or I'll give you a proper beating."

Aunt Polly was so overcome by the splendor of Tom's achievement, that she selected a large, juicy looking apple and handed it to him. And while she was instructing her nephew about the importance of earning a treat instead of stealing or wrongfully getting it, Tom pinched a doughnut.

As he skipped gaily out of the house, Tom saw Sid climbing up the outside stairway that led to the back rooms on the second floor. In a twinkling, the air became full of mud balls and raged around Sid like a hailstorm. Before Aunt Polly could collect her surprised senses and come to Sid's rescue, the boy had been splattered by six or seven mud balls, and Tom was over the fence and gone.

His soul was at peace now that he had settled scores with Sid for calling Aunt Polly's attention to his black thread and getting him into trouble.

Tom was soon safely beyond the reach of capture and punishment. As he was passing by the house where Jeff Thatcher lived, he saw a new girl in the garden—a lovely little blue-eyed creature with yellow hair plaited into two long tails, and wearing a white summer frock.

Tom instantly fell in love with her. A certain Amy Lawrence, whom he had thought he loved

to distraction, vanished out of his heart and left not even a memory of her behind.

Tom now began to 'show off' in all sorts of absurd boyish ways, in order to win the blue-eyed girl's admiration. He turned somersaults, stood on his head, and did all sorts of foolish tricks to impress her. But to his great disappointment, the little girl walked toward the house and went indoors. Poor Tom heaved a great sigh and strode home reluctantly, his head full of all sorts of dreams and plans.

All through supper, Tom's spirits were so high that Aunt Polly wondered what had got into the child? He got a good scolding about splattering Sid with mud balls, but did not seem to mind it in the least. Then he tried to steal sugar from under his aunt's very nose, and got his knuckles rapped for it.

"Aunt, you don't whack Sid when he takes it," Tom complained, quite aggrieved.

"Well, Sid doesn't torture me the way you do!" replied Aunt Polly and went into the kitchen.

Meanwhile Sid, feeling quite victorious, reached for the sugar bowl in a sort of gloating way, which was quite unbearable to Tom. But, Sid's fingers slipped and the bowl dropped and broke.

Tom was in ecstasies now. In such ecstasies, that he even controlled his tongue and was silent. He said to himself that he would not speak a word, even when his aunt came in, but would sit perfectly still till she asked who did the mischief. And then he would tell, and there would be nothing so good in the world as to see that pet model Sid get thrashed.

Tom was so brimming with joy that he could hardly contain himself when Aunt Polly returned and stood above the wrecked sugar bowl, looking furiously from over her spectacles.

'Now it's coming!' Tom said to himself.

And the next instant, he was sprawling on the floor! Aunt Polly had whacked him instead!

"Hold on, now, what are you beating me for? Sid broke it!" groaned Tom.

Aunt Polly paused, puzzled, and Tom looked for healing pity. But when she spoke up again, she only said, "Umf! Well, you didn't get beaten in vain. You must have got into some other mischief when I wasn't around."

Then her conscience reproached her, and she yearned to say something kind and loving to Tom; but she kept silent, and went about her affairs with a troubled heart.

Tom sulked in a corner and glorified his misery. He knew that in her heart his aunt was quite unhappy for having unjustly beaten him, and he was sulkily gratified by it.

Tom started wallowing in self-pity, and pictured himself lying sick with his aunt bending over him, asking him to say one little forgiving word; but he would turn his face to the wall, and die with that word unsaid. Ah, how would Aunt Polly feel then? Then he pictured himself brought home from the river, dead, with his curls all wet, and his sore heart at rest. And then, how his aunt would throw herself upon him, and how her tears would fall and she would pray to God to give her back her boy, and she would never, never ill-treat him any more!

Tom got so worked up with the tragedy of these dreams, that he had to continuously swallow to keep himself from choking. His eyes swam in a blur of water, which overflowed when he winked, and ran down and trickled from the end of his nose. Tom went out of the house and wandered desolately along the dark streets.

About half past nine or ten o'clock, he came before the house where his 'adored unknown' lived. A candle was casting a dull glow upon the curtain of a second-story window.

Tom climbed the fence, threaded his way silently through the plants, till he stood under that window. Then he laid himself down on the ground under the window, upon his back, with his hands clasped upon his breast. And thus, Tom decided, he would die - out in the cold world, with no roof over his homeless head; no loving face to bend pityingly over him when death came. And thus she would find him in the morning, and oh! Would she drop one little tear upon his poor, lifeless form?

At this moment, the window went up, a maidservant's voice shattered the quiet of the night, and a bucketful of water drenched the stretched out sufferer!

CHAPTER 2

Tom Makes Friends V...

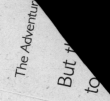

Monday morning found Tom Sawyer miserable. Actually, Monday morning always found him miserable as it began another week's slow suffering in school.

Presently it occurred to Tom that he wished he were sick; then he could stay home from school.

the problem is, sick of what? So, Tom tried find out some probable trace of illness, but no matter how hard he tried, he could find nothing wrong with himself.

Tom investigated again. Suddenly, he discovered that one of his upper front teeth was loose. This was lucky!

Tom was about to begin to groan, when it occurred to him that when his aunt came to know of this, she would pull the tooth out, and that would hurt. So he decided to hold the tooth in reserve for the present, and think of something else. He remembered hearing the doctor tell about a certain illness that laid up a patient for two or three weeks, and threatened to make him lose a finger. So Tom eagerly drew his sore toe from under the bed sheet and held it up for examination. Although he did not know the necessary symptoms, Tom decided to chance it, and began groaning with considerable spirit.

However, Sid slept on, unconscious.

Tom groaned louder, and fancied that he indeed began to feel pain in the toe.

No response from Sid.

Tom was panting with his exertions by now. He rested for a moment, and then began a succession of admirable groans.

Sid snored on!

Tom was irritated. He said, "Sid, Sid!" and shook him.

This seemed to work well. Sid yawned, stretched, then brought himself up on his elbow with a snort, and began to stare at Tom.

Tom went on groaning.

"Tom! Say, Tom!" cried Sid.

No response.

"Here, Tom! Tom! What is the matter, Tom?"

And Sid shook him and looked in his face anxiously.

Tom moaned out, "Oh, don't, Sid. Don't joggle me."

"Why, what's the matter, Tom? I must call auntie."

"No never mind. It'll be over in a while. Maybe! Don't call anybody."

"But I must! Don't groan so, Tom, it's awful. How long you been this way?"

"Hours. Ouch! Oh, don't shake so. Sid, you'll kill me."

"Tom, why didn't you wake me sooner? Oh, Tom, don't! It makes my flesh crawl to hear you. What is the matter?"

"I forgive you everything, Sid. (Groan). Everything you've ever done to me. When I'm gone..."

"Oh, Tom, you aren't dying, are you? Don't, Tom – oh, don't. Maybe ..."

"I forgive everybody, Sid. (Groan). Tell them so. And give my window sash and my cat with one eye to that new girl that's come to town, and tell her..."

But Sid had snatched his clothes and was

gone. He flew downstairs and cried, "Oh, Aunt Polly, come! Tom's dying!"

"Dying!"

"Yes! Don't wait – come quick!"

"Rubbish! I don't believe it!"

But she fled upstairs, nevertheless, with Sid and Mary at her heels. And her face grew white, too, and her lip trembled. When she reached the bedside, she gasped, "Tom! Tom, what's the matter with you? What is the matter with you, child?"

"Oh, auntie, my sore toe is mortified!"

The old lady sank down into a chair and laughed a little, then cried a little, then did both together. This made her feel better and she said, "Tom, what a shock you gave me! Now you shut up that nonsense and climb out of the bed."

The groans ceased and the pain vanished from the toe. The boy felt a little foolish, and he said, "Aunt Polly, the toe did hurt so much that I never minded my tooth at all."

"Your tooth, indeed! What's the matter with your tooth?"

"One of them is loose, and it aches awfully."

"There, there, now, don't begin that groaning again. Open your mouth. Well – your tooth is loose, but you're not going to die because of that. Mary, get me a silk thread, and a chunk of fire out of the kitchen stove."

"Oh, please, auntie, don't pull it out!" cried Tom. "It doesn't hurt any more. Please don't, auntie. I don't want to stay away from school."

"Oh, that means all this row was created by you because you didn't want to go to school? Tom, Tom, I love you so much, and yet you are always breaking my old heart with all your silly pranks."

By this time, all the dental instruments were ready. The old lady looped one end of the silk thread to Tom's tooth, and tied the other end to the bedpost. Then she seized the chunk of fire and suddenly thrust it almost into the boy's face.

Tom at once jumped back, and the next moment, his tooth was dangling by the bedpost.

As Tom trudged towards his school after breakfast, the gap in the upper row of his teeth was the envy of every boy he met on the way. Shortly after, he met the village outcast– Huckleberry Finn. Huck was the son of the town drunkard, and was hated as well as dreaded by all the mothers of the village because he was idle and lawless. But all the children admired him so and wanted to be like him.

Tom, like the rest of the boys, envied Huck's freedom and lack of propriety. Huck was always dressed in rags or cast-off clothes. His hat was wide and lopped out of its brim; his coat hung nearly to his heels; only one suspender supported his trousers; the seat of the trousers bagged low, and the fringed legs dragged in the dirt when not rolled up. Huckleberry came and went at his own free will. He slept on doorsteps; he did not have to go to school or to church, or obey anybody;

he could go fishing or swimming when and where he chose, and stay as long as it suited him; nobody forbade him to fight; he could sit up as late as he pleased; he never had to wash, nor put on clean clothes; he could swear wonderfully. In a word, Huck had everything that makes life precious and worthwhile.

Tom greeted the outcast:

"Hello, Huckleberry!"

"Hello yourself, and see how you like this."

"What's that?"

"It's a dead cat."

"Say, what are dead cats good for, Huck?"

"Cats can cure warts."

"No! Is that so? Say, Hucky, when are you going to try the cat?"

"Tonight. I think the spirits will come after old Hoss Williams tonight, who was buried last Saturday."

"Let me go with you?"

"Of course, if you aren't afraid."

"Afraid! It isn't likely. Will you meow?"

"Yes - and you meow back. Last time, you kept me meowing till I was showered with stones."

"I won't. I couldn't meow that night because auntie was watching me, but I'll meow this time. Say – what's that?"

"Just a tick."

"What'll you take for him?"

"I don't know. I don't want to sell him."

"Say, Huck, I'll give you my tooth for him."

"Let's see it."

Tom got out a bit of paper and carefully unrolled it. Huckleberry viewed the precious tooth it held wistfully. The temptation was very strong.

At last he asked, "Is it genuine?"

Tom lifted his lip and showed the vacancy.

"Well, all right," said Huckleberry, "it's a trade."

Tom enclosed the tick in the percussion-cap box, (a small box where explosive powder is kept) and the boys separated, each feeling wealthier than before.

When Tom reached his school, he strode in briskly, hung his hat on a peg and flung himself into his seat with business-like rapidity. The class teacher was dozing away in his great splint-bottom armchair. The interruption roused him.

"Thomas Sawyer!"

Tom knew that when his name was pronounced in full, it meant trouble.

"Sir!"

"Come up here. Now, sir, why are you late again, as usual?"

Tom was about to take the help of a lie, when he saw two long tails of yellow hair hanging down a back that he recognized instantly; and by that form was the only vacant place on the girls' side of the room.

He instantly said, "I stopped to talk with Huckleberry Finn!"

The master stared speechlessly and helplessly at Tom. The buzz of study ceased. The pupils wondered if this foolhardy boy had lost his mind.

"You - you did what?" said the class teacher, finally.

"I stopped to talk with Huckleberry Finn."

There was no mistaking the words.

"Thomas Sawyer, this is the most astounding confession I have ever listened to. Take off your jacket."

The teacher generously whipped Tom's back until he was tired.

"Now, sir, go and sit with the girls!" he ordered Tom. "And let this be a warning to you."

Tom sat down upon the pine bench amidst an outburst of titter that went round the classroom. Nudges and winks passed through the room, but Tom sat still and seemed to study his book. Soon however, the attention of the other children diverted to other matters and Tom stole stealthy glances at his sweetheart. Then he presented her with a nice, ripe peach. But she thrust it away. He thrust it towards her again. And again she pushed it away, but a little less reluctantly. The third time he placed it in front of her, she quietly took it. Now, emboldened by her acceptance, Tom began to draw something on his slate, hiding his work with his left hand. For a time, the girl seemed not to notice. But after a while, her curiosity got the better of her and she whispered, "Let me see it."

Tom showed her a shabby drawing of a house with a corkscrew of smoke coming out of it.

The girl gazed at the drawing for a moment, and then said, "It's nice. Now make a man."

So Tom drew a man's figure, larger in size than the house itself.

However the girl was not too fussy and was satisfied with Tom's drawing.

"It's a beautiful man," she declared. "Now draw me coming along."

So, Tom drew an hourglass with a full moon on top, straw limbs on the sides, and armed the spreading fingers with an impressive fan.

"It's ever so nice—I wish I could draw."

"It's easy," whispered Tom, "I'll teach you. What's your name?"

"Becky Thatcher. What's yours? Oh, I know. It's Thomas Sawyer."

"That's the name they call me when they have to beat me. But I'm Tom when I'm good. You call me Tom."

Now Tom began to scrawl something on the slate, hiding the words from the girl. But she at once begged to see what it was.

"No, you'll tell," said Tom.

"No I won't - deed and deed and double deed, I won't."

"You won't tell anybody at all? Ever, as long as you live?"

"No, I won't ever tell anybody."

So, Tom pretended to reluctantly show her the slate on which the following words were written: "I love you."

"Oh, you bad thing!" cried the girl and rapped

Tom's hand, but she turned red and looked pleased, nevertheless.

Just then, Tom felt a painful pull on his ear, and the next instant he was tugged by the ear across the room to his own seat by the class teacher. But although Tom's ear tingled, his heart was jubilant.

CHAPTER 3

Tom Is Heart-Broken

The more Tom tried to concentrate on his books, the more his mind wandered. It seemed to him that recess would never come. Tom's heart ached to be free, or else to have something interesting to do to pass the time. His hand wandered into his pocket and the percussion-cap box came out. Tom released the tick and put it on his desk. Immediately, the till then captive creature began to move in one direction. Tom turned the tick aside with a pin and made it take a new direction.

Tom's best friend, Joe Harper, who was sitting next to him, instantly got interested in this entertaining sport. He, too, took out a pin and began to help Tom in exercising the tick. Soon, Tom declared that they were interfering with each other. So he put Joe's slate on the desk and drew a line down the middle of it from top to bottom.

"Now," said he, "as long as the tick is on your side you can move him, but if he gets to my side you've got to leave him alone."

Joe agreed and the two boys resumed their game. After a while, the tick escaped from Tom and crossed the line to Joe's side. Then, after being harassed by Joe, the tick again crossed back to Tom's side. This change of base occurred for quite some time. The two boys bowed their heads together over the tick and pestered the poor creature so much, that it got quite agitated and constantly moved from one side to the other. But finally, it got tired and seemed to linger on Joe's side.

At last, Tom could stand it no longer. He reached out to Joe's side of the slate to move the tick with his pin. At this, Joe became angry.

"Leave it alone, Tom!" he shouted.

"Look here, Joe Harper, whose tick is that?" replied Tom, equally hotly.

"I don't care whose tick it is – it's on my side of the slate and you shan't touch it!"

"I'll do whatever I want with it!"

Just then, a tremendous smack fell on Tom's back, and then its duplicate on Joe's.

The boys had been so absorbed in their fight that they hadn't noticed the hush that had fallen upon the class as the teacher had come tiptoeing down the room and stood over them. He had watched a good part of their interesting game, and then had contributed his own part by giving them some good quality whacking.

When school broke up at noon, Tom and Becky Thatcher stayed back. They sat together, with Tom drawing another surprise house for Becky on his slate.

After a while, when their interest in drawing had lessened, Tom asked Becky, "Do you love rats?"

"No! I hate them. But I like chewing gum."

"Oh, I do too! I wish I had some now."

"I have got some. I'll let you chew it for a while, but you must give it back to me."

The matter was settled and the two chewed the gum in turns, and happily dangled their legs against the bench.

"Say – Becky, were you ever engaged?" asked Tom.

"No; what's that?" Becky asked.

"Why, you only have to tell a boy that you

won't ever, ever love anyone but him, and then you kiss, and that is all. Anybody can do it."

"Kiss? What do you kiss for?"

"Well, they always do that."

After a great deal of persuasion, Becky agreed to it, and Tom happily kissed her.

"Now Becky you will never love anybody but me, and never marry anybody but me," said Tom. "And that's only part of it! When we're walking home, you are to walk with me, and we choose each other at parties, because that's the way you do when you are engaged."

"It's so nice," exclaimed Becky. "I never heard of it before!"

"Oh, it's ever so good! Why, me and Amy Lawrence…"

It was already too late. Tom understood his mistake a fraction too late. Becky's large eyes filled with tears.

"Oh, Tom! Then I am not the first you've ever been engaged to!"

And she started to cry.

"Oh, don't cry, Becky, I don't care for her any more."

Tom tried to put his arm around Becky's shoulders to calm her down. But she pushed him away, turned her face to the wall, and went on crying.

Tom felt offended, got up and walked away from the sobbing girl. For a while he marched restlessly about, but then he realized that the mistake was his and so went back to Becky.

He took out his chief treasure, a brass knob from his pocket, and offered it to Becky.

"Please, Becky, won't you take it?" he said.

Becky threw the brass knob on the floor. Tom at once marched out of the school. He went over the hills and even further beyond, and did not return to school that day.

Soon, Becky began to regret her actions and started searching the entire playground for Tom. But he was nowhere to be found. Finally, Becky gave up her search. Her heart was broken, and she sat down crying and reproaching herself.

Tom wandered through lanes and by lanes till he entered a dense wood. There he sat gloomily under a mossy tree. What wrong had he done? Nothing! He had meant the best in the world for Becky and she had treated him like a dog – yes, just like a dog. She would be sorry one day but it would be too late then!

Oh! If only he could die temporarily!

Tom began to wonder what it would be like if he went away to unknown lands, far beyond the seas, and never came back again! How would she feel then?

Tom had just decided that he would run away from home and become a pirate, when he saw his friend Joe Harper coming towards him. Soon, the two boys decided to play Robin Hood and began a fight armed with stick swords.

After quite a long, fierce battle Tom shouted, "Fall down! Why don't you fall down?"

"I shan't!" replied Joe. "Why don't you fall yourself?"

"It's your turn to fall," pointed out Tom.

Joe had to agree and obediently fell down on the ground.

So, the game went on, and finally, during dinnertime, the boys bid each other goodbye and proceeded homewards.

CHAPTER 4

Murder!

At half past nine that night, after dinner, Tom and Sid went to bed as usual. They said their prayers, and soon Sid was fast asleep. Tom lay awake, restless and impatient. The clock went on ticking endlessly, the beams cracked, the stairs creaked, and a muffled snore came from Aunt Polly's room. Finally, just as he had started to doze off, there came the sound of a melancholy 'meow'. The raising of a neighboring window awakened Tom completely. There was a soft 'meow' again. Immediately after that, he heard a cry of 'Shoo! You pest!' followed by the crash of an empty bottle.

Tom jumped out of the bed, dressed himself, and was out of the window – onto the ground – in the twinkling of an eye. He whispered 'meow' once or twice as he moved cautiously ahead. He found Huckleberry Finn waiting for him with his dead cat.

Together, the boys set off towards the graveyard that was at a distance of about one and a half miles from the village.

After walking for about half an hour, the boys reached the old graveyard atop a hill. Grass and weed grew all over the place. All the old graves were sunken in and not one tombstone could be seen.

A faint wind moaned through the trees, and

Tom was afraid that it was the spirits of the dead showing displeasure at being disturbed.

The two boys talked little - and that too in whispers. Soon, they found the grave they were looking for, and placed themselves beside a cluster of three elm trees that grew within a feet of the grave.

Then they waited in silence for what seemed a long time.

"Hucky, do you think the dead people would like us being here?" whispered Tom.

"I wish I knew. It's awful solemn, isn't it?" Huckleberry whispered back.

The two became silent for a moment. After a while, Tom seized Huck's arm and whispered, "Shhh…"

"What is it Tom?" murmured Huck, and the two boys huddled together with beating hearts.

"Sh! There it is again! Didn't you hear it?"

"Lord, Tom, they're coming! They're coming, sure. What'll we do?"

"I don't know! Think they'll see us?"

"Oh, Tom, they can see in the dark. I wish I hadn't come."

The boys bent their heads together and hardly breathed. A muffled sound of voices floated up from the far end of the graveyard.

"Oh, don't be afraid," Tom tried to soothe his friend. "We aren't doing any harm. If we keep perfectly still, maybe they won't notice us at all."

Some vague figures were approaching towards them through the gloom, swinging an old-fashioned tin lantern. Presently Huckleberry whispered with a shudder, "It's the devils sure enough; three of them!"

"Don't be afraid. They aren't going to hurt us."

"Sh!"

"What is it, Huck?"

"They're humans! One of them is, anyway. He has old Muff Potter's voice. He is drunk as usual."

"Say - Huck, I recognize another of the voices," put in Tom, "it's Injun Joe."

"Yes! So it is," replied Huck. "I wonder what they are up to."

The boys kept quiet and sat very still, for the three figures had now reached the grave and stood within a few feet of where the boys were hiding.

"Here it is," said the third voice; and the owner of it held the lantern up and revealed the face of young Doctor Robinson.

Potter and Injun Joe now started digging up the grave with shovels. The doctor put the lantern at the head of the grave and came and sat down with his back against one of the elm trees.

"Hurry, men!" he said, in a low voice. "The moon might come out at any moment."

The diggers growled in response and went on digging, till one of the spades struck something with a dull, woody sound. In another moment, the two men had hoisted up a coffin on the ground.

They forced open the lid of the coffin with their shovels, got out the body and dumped it rudely on the ground. The corpse was then placed on the wheelbarrow, covered with a blanket and tied down with a rope. Potter cut off the ends with a spring knife.

"Now it is ready," said Injun Joe. "Another five dollars more or here it stays."

"Look here, what does this mean?" said the doctor. "I've paid you in advance."

"Yes, and you done more than that," said Injun Joe, approaching the doctor. "Five years ago, you drove me away from your father's house one night, when I came to ask for something to eat. Your father even had me jailed for a vagrant. Then I swore I'd get my revenge one day, and I haven't forgotten my vow. Today, I've got you, and I'll settle scores!"

The doctor struck out suddenly and knocked Injun Joe to the ground. Muff Potter dropped his knife, and exclaimed, "Here, now, don't you hit my pal!"

The next moment he jumped on the doctor and the two began wrestling with each other on the ground.

In the meantime, Injun Joe sprang to his feet, his eyes flaming with passion, and snatched up Potter's knife. Round and round he went about the fighters, seeking an opportunity to strike. All at once, the doctor flung himself free and knocked down Potter to the ground; in the same instant, Joe saw his chance and drove the knife into the doctor's chest.

The doctor reeled and fell upon Potter, flooding him with his blood.

At the same instant, the clouds blotted out the dreadful scene, and the two frightened boys went speeding away in the dark.

The doctor groaned, gave a long gasp and breathed his last.

Injun Joe muttered, "The score is settled now."

Then he searched the doctor's pockets and

took out his purse and other belongings. Next he put the fatal knife in Potter's open right hand, and sat down upon the coffin. After a few minutes, Potter began to stir and moan. His hand closed on the knife. He raised it, glanced at it, and dropped it with a shudder.

"Lord, how did this happen, Joe?" he asked, confusedly.

Injun Joe told him that while he and the two were fighting and the doctor had given him a head blow, Potter had got up the very next moment and had stabbed the doctor with his knife.

Potter trembled and grew white.

"I can't remember anything! Tell me, Joe - honest, now, old fellow, did I do it? Joe, I never meant to – upon my honor, I never meant to, Joe. Oh, it's awful; he was so young and promising! I have always stood up for you, Joe; say you won't tell anybody."

And the poor creature dropped on his knees

before the cold-hearted murderer, and clasped his hands in appeal.

"All right, I won't tell," replied the lying criminal. "Come now, this isn't any time for blubbering. You go off that way and I'll go this."

And the two men went away in opposite directions. All that was left to remind one of the terrible events of that night were the murdered man, the blanketed corpse, the lidless coffin, and the open grave.

The two boys ran on and on toward the village, speechless with horror. From time to time they anxiously glanced over their shoulders as if afraid they might be followed. Finally, they reached the old tannery of the village, burst through its open door, and fell panting on the ground. Eventually, when their pulses slowed down, Tom whispered, "Huckleberry, what do you think will happen?"

"If Doctor Robinson dies, I think there will be a hanging."

The two boys soon came to the conclusion

that they were the only ones who had witnessed the murder of the doctor, as Muff Potter had been out cold! But if they told about it, and then supposing Injun Joe didn't hang, then he'd surely kill them both!

"Now, look-a-here, Tom, let us swear to one another to keep mum."

"I agree," said Tom. "It's the best thing. Let's hold hands and swear that ..."

"Oh no," interrupted Huck, "for a big thing like this we need to write it down on paper – with blood!"

Tom heartily approved the idea. He picked up a piece of bark that lay in the moonlight, and scrawled out the following lines:

HUCK FINN AND TOM SAWYER SWEARS
THEY WILL KEEP MUM ABOUT THIS
AND THEY WISH THEY MAY
DROP DOWN DEAD IN THEIR TRACKS
IF THEY EVER TELL AND ROT.

Then the two pricked their fingers and signed their initials in blood. Next, they buried the bark close to the wall, with some gloomy ceremonies and chants, and repeated the oath that their lips were sealed for ever!

Finally, the two boys separated, each brooding over the recent terrible incidents. When Tom crept in at his bedroom window, the night was almost over. He undressed carefully, and fell asleep, congratulating himself that nobody knew of his escapade. He was not aware that the gently snoring Sid was awake, and had been so for an hour.

CHAPTER 5

Tom's Guilty Conscience

When Tom awoke, Sid was dressed and gone. The day had broken long before. Tom was alarmed. Why had he not been called — scolded till he was up, as usual? Within five minutes Tom had dressed and had gone downstairs, feeling sore and drowsy.

The family had finished breakfast but they were still seated at the table.

After breakfast his aunt took him aside, and Tom almost brightened in the hope that he was going to be flogged. But it was not so. His aunt wept and asked him how could he go on breaking her old heart so?

"Go and ruin yourself Tom," sobbed Aunt Polly. "Bring my gray hairs with sorrow to the grave. I know it is no use for me to even try any more!"

This was worse than a thousand whippings! Tom's heart was sorer now than his body. He cried, he pleaded, and promised to reform over and over again.

When he received his dismissal, Tom felt that he had won only a half-hearted forgiveness and established only a half-hearted confidence.

Tom felt so miserable that any thought of revenge towards Sid did not occur, thus making the latter's prompt retreat through the back gate quite unnecessary. He moped to school gloomy and sad, and quietly took his flogging, along with Joe Harper, for playing hooky the day before. Then he sat down in his usual seat with his elbows on the desk and his jaws in his hands, and stared at the wall blankly. At that point he felt his elbow pressing against some hard substance. Tom saw that it was something rolled in a paper. He picked it up and unrolled it. A long, lingering, sigh followed, and his heart broke. It was his brass and iron knob!

The one he had gifted to Becky Thatcher.

By noon, the entire village was stunned by the news of the horrible murder. The story flew from man to man and house to house with almost telegraphic speed. Of course the schoolmaster gave the children holiday for that afternoon; and if he hadn't done that, the town would have thought him a strange person indeed!

A bloody knife had been found close to the murdered man, and it had been recognized by somebody as belonging to Muff Potter – so the story ran.

The entire town was drifting toward the graveyard. Tom's heartbreak over Becky Thatcher vanished, and he joined the procession. When he arrived at the dreadful place, he wormed his small body through the crowd and stared at the disturbing scene ahead. Suddenly, somebody pinched his arm. He turned, and his eyes met Huckleberry's. At once both looked elsewhere, and wondered if anybody had noticed anything in their mutual glance. But everybody was talking, and intent upon the horrifying spectacle before them.

"Poor young fellow!"

"This ought to be a lesson to grave - robbers!"

"Muff Potter will hang for this if they catch him!"

In the midst of all this, Tom's eyes fell on Injun Joe who was standing impassively amongst the crowd; Tom shivered from head to toe. At this moment the crowd began to sway and struggle, and voices shouted, "It's him! It's him! He's coming himself!"

"Who? Who?" cried twenty voices together.

"Muff Potter!"

The crowd separated now and the sheriff came through, officiously leading Potter by the arm. The poor fellow's face was haggard and pale. When finally he stood before the murdered man, he started trembling and, putting his face in his hands, he burst into tears.

Then, as Huckleberry and Tom stood dumbstruck, the stonehearted liar Injun Joe calmly described to the Sheriff how Muff Potter had stabbed the doctor during a drunken rage. Listening to Injun Joe's lies, the two stunned boys felt that God's lightning would surely fall upon his head any moment.

However, they stuck to their pledge, and kept mum.

Yet Tom's conscience kept pricking him and disturbing his sleep for a week after this.

One morning, while the family was at breakfast, Sid complained, "Tom, you toss about and talk in your sleep, and keep me awake half the time."

Tom grew pale and dropped his eyes.

"It's a bad sign," said Aunt Polly, solemnly. "What's on your mind, Tom?"

"Nothing," said Tom. But his hand shook so much, that he spilled his coffee.

"And last night you said, 'It's blood,' and 'don't torment me or I'll tell'," said Sid. "What is it you'll tell?"

Luckily, Aunt Polly unknowingly came to Tom's relief.

"Shoo! Now I know what the matter is!" said she. "It's that dreadful murder. I dream about it almost every night myself. Sometimes I dream it's me who has done it!"

Sid seemed satisfied with this explanation and Tom escaped from the room as quickly as possible. After that, he complained of toothache for a week, and tied up his jaws every night. He was ignorant of the fact that Sid watched him each night, and frequently slipped off the bandage and lay listening to his mutterings. Then he slipped the bandage back to its place again. If Sid really managed to make anything out of Tom's incoherent mutterings, he kept it to himself.

During this time, Tom often went to the small little brick jail that stood on the edge of the marsh at the end of the village. Through the grated jail-window Tom would smuggle such small gifts to Muff Potter as he could get hold of. These offerings greatly helped to ease Tom's conscience.

CHAPTER 6

The Experiment With Painkiller

One of the reasons why Tom's mind could drift away from its secret troubles was that it had found a new and weighty matter to interest itself about. Becky Thatcher had stopped coming to school!

Initially, Tom had tried not to think much about her, but had failed. He began to find himself hanging around her house, watching her window at nights, and feeling very miserable. Becky was ill. What if she should die!

Poor Tom no longer took an interest in war, nor even in piracy. The charm of life was gone, and nothing was left but misery. Tom put his hoop and bat away, as there was no joy in them any more.

Aunt Polly became worried to see her nephew like this. She began to try all types of cures on him. Aunt Polly was a firm believer in all novel methods of treatment, and a subscriber to all the 'health' periodicals. A simple-hearted person, she had enormous faith in whatever was mentioned in these magazines. So, gathering together her quack periodicals and her quack medicines, she began Tom's cure.

First she tried the water treatment. Each morning she drowned him with a deluge of cold water; then scrubbed him down with a towel, then rolled him up in a wet sheet, and finally put him away under blankets till she had sweated his soul clean.

Yet despite all this, Tom grew more and more melancholy, and dejected. Aunt Polly now tried hot baths, shower baths, and plunges; but that did not work either, nor did the slim oatmeal diet and blister plasters. But what alarmed Aunt Polly most of all was Tom's total indifference to all this. He did not resist or try his usual antics, but bore everything blankly. This indifference just had to be broken up!

It was then that Aunt Polly came to know about something called 'painkiller'. She immediately ordered a lot of it. She tasted it and was filled with gratitude. It was simply fire in a liquid form! Aunt Polly dropped the water treatment and everything else, and fixed her faith to the painkiller. She gave Tom a teaspoonful and waited anxiously for the result.

Her troubles were instantly at rest and her soul at peace again, for Tom's indifference instantly vanished! He started taking an unusual interest in the medicine.

Actually, by this time Tom had started getting bored of this kind of life. So after considering various plans for relief, he finally thought of pretending to be fond of painkiller. Tom asked for it so often that he became a nuisance, and Aunt Polly had to tell him to help himself and stop bothering her. Little did she know that Tom was actually mending a crack in the sitting room floor with the medicine!

One day, Tom was in the act of dosing the crack, when his aunt's yellow cat came along, purring, eying the teaspoon greedily, and begging for a taste.

"Don't ask for it unless you want it, Peter," said Tom.

But Peter indicated that he did want it.

"You better be sure."

Peter was sure.

"Now that you've asked for it, I'll give it to you. But if you don't like it, you mustn't blame anybody but your own self."

Peter was satisfied. So Tom pried his mouth open and poured down the painkiller. Peter sprang a couple of yards in the air, delivered a war whoop and set off round and round the room, banging against furniture, upsetting flowerpots, and creating universal disaster.

Aunt Polly entered in time to see Peter throw a few double somersaults, deliver a final mighty hurrah, and sail through the open window carrying the rest of the flowerpots with him.

The old lady stood amazed, peering over her glasses, while Tom lay on the floor almost dying with laughter.

"Tom, what on earth is the matter with that cat?"

"I don't know, Aunt Polly," gasped Tom. "Cats always act so when they're having a good time."

But Aunt Polly was already bending down,

and picked up the handle of the teaspoon that was visible under the bed drapes. Tom winced, and dropped his eyes.

Aunt Polly raised him by his ear and said, "Now, sir, why did you treat that poor dumb animal so?"

"I did it out of pity because he hadn't any aunt."

"Hadn't any aunt! You blockhead, what has that got to do with it?"

"Heaps! Because if he'd had one, she would have burnt his bowels with her cures without any thought!"

Aunt Polly felt a sudden pang of remorse. This was putting the thing in a new light; what was cruelty to a cat might be cruelty to a boy, too.

She put her hand on Tom's head and said gently, "I meant for the best, Tom. And Tom, it did do you good."

Tom looked up in her face and said gravely, "I know you meant for the best, aunty, and so did I

for Peter. It did him good, too. I never saw him get around so since..."

"Oh, run along, Tom, before you annoy me again. And try and see if you can't be a good boy, for once."

Tom Sawyer reached his school early – an incident highly unusual, but something that was happening every day these days. And instead of playing with his friends, he hung about the gate of the schoolyard, and watched and watched for an arrival. At last his patience paid off and Becky Thatcher walked in!

Tom's heart gave a great bound. The next instant he was shouting, laughing, chasing boys, jumping over the fence, standing on his head – doing all the heroic things he could think of. And all the time he kept throwing secret glances at Becky Thatcher to see if she was noticing.

However, Becky seemed to be unconscious of it all; she never even looked. Tom carried his gymnastics even nearer to her; he snatched a boy's cap, hurled it to the roof of the schoolhouse, broke through a group of boys, and fell sprawling under Becky's nose, almost upsetting her.

Becky turned, and said with her nose in the air, "Mf! Some people think they're mighty smart – always showing off!"

Tom's cheeks burned. He picked himself up and crept away, crushed and crest-fallen.

Tom had made up his mind. He was a forsaken, friendless boy, and nobody loved him. Now he had no choice but to lead a life of crime. Yes, that's what he would do. Lead a life of crime!

By this time he had left the school far behind, and the school bell tinkled faintly in his ears. He sobbed to think he should never, never hear that old familiar sound any more.

Just at this point he met his friend, Joe Harper, sad and miserable, and with a great and gloomy purpose in his heart. His mother had whipped him for drinking some cream that he had never even tasted! It was plain to Joe that his mother was tired of him and wished him to go. Joe had thus come away from home into the unfeeling world to suffer and die.

As the two distressed boys walked along, they made a deal to stick by each other and be brothers and never separate till death. Then they began to lay their plans for the future. After much discussion, they finally decided to run away and become pirates.

Tom declared that 'Jackson Island' would be the perfect hideout for them. It was a long, narrow, uninhabited forestland, about three miles below St. Petersburg on the Mississippi river. He and Joe then hunted up Huckleberry Finn to join them in this adventure. Huck was as always more than ready for any adventures, and promptly agreed to the proposal.

The three boys decided to meet at a lonely spot on the riverbank at midnight. There was a small log raft there, which they meant to capture. Each would bring hooks and lines, and such food and provisions as he could steal.

Around midnight, Tom arrived with boiled ham and a few other supplies at the scheduled meeting place. It was a starry night, and very still. The mighty river lay silent, like an ocean. Tom listened a moment, but no sound disturbed the quiet. Then he gave a low, distinct whistle. There was an answering whistle. Tom whistled twice more. It was answered in the same way. Then a guarded voice said, "Who goes there?"

"Tom Sawyer the Black Avenger of the Spanish Main. Now tell your names."

"Huck Finn the Red-Handed, and Joe Harper the Terror of the Seas."

It was Tom who had furnished these titles from his favorite literature.

"It's all right. Now give the countersign."

Two hoarse whispers delivered the same awful word in chorus:

"BLOOD!"

The three adventurers now came forward and loaded their provisions onto a small raft tied up on the bank. The Terror of the Seas had brought a side of bacon, while Finn the Red-Handed had stolen a skillet and some leaf tobacco. He had also brought a few corncobs to make pipes with.

Soon, the three shoved off, with Tom in command, Huck at the after oar and Joe at the forward. About two o'clock in the morning, the raft grounded two hundred yards above the head of the island. The boys waded back and forth until they had landed their goods. Part of the little raft's belongings consisted of an old sail, and this they spread over a nook in the bushes as a tent to shelter their provisions. However, the boys themselves decided to sleep in the open air, as befitted outlaws.

They built a fire against the side of a great log, deep within the forest, and then cooked some bacon in the frying pan for supper. To be feasting in that wild, free way in an unexplored and uninhabited island, far, far away from the haunts of men, was fascinating indeed! The three unanimously declared that they never would return to civilization.

When the last crisp slice of bacon was gone, the boys stretched themselves out on the grass, happy and content - and drifted off to a deep sleep.

CHAPTER 7

Declared Dead!

When Tom awoke in the morning, he wondered where he was! He sat up and rubbed his eyes and looked around. It was quite a while before he recollected everything.

Joe and Huck still slept. Tom stirred up the two pirates, and they all clattered away with a shout. In a minute or two they had stripped and were chasing and tumbling over each other in the clear shallow waters.

They returned to their camp wonderfully refreshed, and extremely hungry. Soon, they had the campfire blazing up again. While Joe was slicing bacon for breakfast, Tom and Huck asked him to hold on a minute. They went to a nook in the riverbank and threw in their fishing lines and soon returned with quite a catch. They fried the fish with the bacon, and no fish had ever seemed so delicious before.

After breakfast they lay for a while in the shade, and then went off through the woods on an exploring expedition. They tramped gaily along, over decaying logs, and through tangled underbrush. Now and then they came upon snug nooks carpeted with grass and jeweled with flowers.

They discovered that the island was about three miles long and a quarter of a mile wide, and that the nearest shore was separated from it only by a narrow channel hardly two hundred yards wide. It was almost the middle of the afternoon when they got back to camp. They were too tired to stop and fish, but they feasted lavishly upon cold ham, and then threw themselves down in the shade to talk. But the talk soon began to drag, and then died.

Gradually, the stillness of the woods, and the sense of loneliness began to fall upon the spirits of the boys. Soon, the boys realized that it was a budding sense of homesickness they were experiencing. Even Huck was dreaming of his doorsteps and empty hogsheads. But all three were ashamed of their weakness, and none was brave enough to speak of his feelings.

For some time, now, the boys had been conscious of a peculiar sound in the distance, which now became more pronounced. The boys started, glanced at each other, and then tried to listen intently. There was a long silence; then a deep, sullen boom came floating down out of the distance.

"What is it?" exclaimed Joe, under his breath.

"Shh!" said Tom. "Listen, don't talk."

They waited for a time that seemed almost an age, and then the same muffled boom resounded through the solemn hush.

"Let's go and see."

The boys sprang to their feet and hurried to the shore toward the town. They parted the bushes on the bank, and peered out over the water. A little steam ferryboat was about a mile below the village, drifting with the current. Her broad deck seemed crowded with people. There were many small boats rowing about in the neighborhood of the ferryboat, but the boys could not find out what the men in them were doing. Presently, a great jet of white smoke burst from the ferryboat's side, and that same dull throb of sound was heard again.

"I know now!" exclaimed Tom. "Somebody's drowned!"

"That's it!" said Huck. "They did that last summer when Bill Turner got drowned. They say, when a cannon ball is shot over the water, it makes the body come up to the top."

"I wish I was over there, now," said Joe.

"I do too," said Huck. "I'd give heaps to know who is drowned."

As the boys watched, a revealing thought flashed through Tom's mind.

"Boys, I know who's drowned!" he exclaimed. "It's us!"

The three boys felt like heroes at once. They were missed; they were mourned; hearts were breaking on their account; tears were being shed; memories of unkindness meted out to them were rising up; and best of all, they were the talk of the whole town, and the envy of all the boys.

It was worthwhile to be a pirate after all!

As twilight drew on, the ferryboat went back to the town and the little boats disappeared. The pirates too returned to camp, feeling jubilant with pride. They caught fish, cooked supper and ate it, and then fell to guessing at what the village was thinking and saying about them. But as the night closed in, they gradually ceased to talk and sat gazing into the fire, with their minds evidently wandering elsewhere. The excitement was gone now, and Tom and Joe began thinking of the people back home, who were not enjoying their play at all. They started growing troubled and unhappy and a sigh or two escaped, unawares.

By and by, Joe timidly suggested that they might consider a return home; not right now, but…

Tom laughed at him scornfully, and Huck too joined in with him. And so, the matter was effectually laid to rest for the moment.

As the night deepened, Huck and Joe soon lay snoring. Tom lay upon his elbow, motionless for some time - watching the two intently. At last, he got up cautiously, tiptoed his way among the trees till he was out of hearing, and immediately broke into a run in the direction of the sandbar.

At first, Tom waded through the water towards the Illinois shore. And then, when wading was no longer possible, he swam the remaining hundred yards and finally reached the shore. Then he ran through the woods, following the shore, with streaming garments. Shortly before ten o'clock, he came out into an open place opposite the village, and saw the ferryboat lying in the shadow of the trees. Everything was quiet under the twinkling stars. Tom crept down the bank, slipped into the water, swam three or four strokes, climbed into the boat, laid himself down under a seat, and waited, panting.

Presently a voice gave the order to 'cast off' the boat. A minute or two later the voyage had begun. Tom felt happy in his success, for he knew it was the boat's last trip for the night. After twelve or fifteen minutes the boat reached the shore, and Tom quietly slipped overboard.

He flew along the streets and alleys, and shortly found himself at his aunt's back fence.

He climbed over it, and looking in at the sitting room window, saw a light was burning there. Aunt Polly, Sid, Mary, and Joe Harper's mother were sitting together, talking. They were near the bed, and the bed was between them and the door. Tom went to the door and softly lifted up the latch. Then he pressed gently and the door yielded a crack. Tom continued pushing cautiously, till there was enough space for him to squeeze through.

"But as I said," Aunt Polly was saying, "he wasn't bad, only mischievous. He never meant any harm, and he was the best-hearted boy that ever was;" and she began to cry.

"It was just so with my Joe, always up to every kind of mischief, but he was just as unselfish and kind as he could be, and to think I went and whipped him for taking that cream, never once recollecting that I threw it out myself because it was sour! Now will I see him again in this world? Never, never, never, poor abused boy!"

And Mrs. Harper sobbed as if her heart would break.

"I hope Tom's better off where he is now," said Sid. "But if he had been better in some ways …"

"SID!" Aunt Polly almost shouted. "Not a word against my Tom! God will take care of him! Oh, he was such a comfort to me, although he tormented my old heart so. But he's out of all his troubles now…"

This memory was too much for the old lady, and she broke down completely. Tom was snuffling now, himself, more in self-pity than anything else. Still, he was sufficiently touched by his aunt's grief to want to rush out from under the bed and overwhelm her with joy, but he resisted and lay still.

He went on listening and realized that initially he and his two friends were thought drowned while swimming. Then the small raft had been missed, and people had decided that the boys had gone down the river on that raft, and would presently turn up at the next town. But toward noon the raft had been found – and thus, that hope too died. It was then concluded that the boys had been drowned; otherwise hunger would have driven them home by nightfall. The search for the bodies too had been made, but in vain. This was Wednesday night. If the bodies continued missing until Sunday, all hope would be given over, and the funerals would be conducted that morning.

Tom shuddered to hear this news.

Mrs. Harper bid a sobbing goodnight to Aunt Polly. Then the two flung themselves into each other's arms and had a good, consoling cry, and then parted. Sid too snuffled a bit, and Mary went off crying with all her heart.

Aunt Polly knelt down and prayed for Tom so touchingly, and with such measureless love in her old trembling voice that Tom was drenched in tears again.

Aunt Polly kept tossing and turning restlessly

for some time. But at last she was still, only moaning a little in her sleep. Now Tom crept out of the bed, shaded the candlelight with his hand, and stood looking at his aunt. His heart was full of pity for her. He took out a sycamore bark from his pocket, placed it near the candle and began to write. Then he thought of something and his face lighted with a happy smile. He quickly put the bark in his pocket, bent over and kissed Aunt Polly, and stealthily went out of the room, latching the door behind him.

It was broad daylight by the time Tom returned to Jackson's Island. As he reached their camp, he was received gladly by his friends.

As the boys feasted on a sumptuous breakfast of bacon and fish, Tom recounted his adventures. The two felt like heroes by the time Tom had finished his story. Then Tom lay down in a shady nook to sleep till noon, while the other pirates got ready to fish and explore.

Later, the gang went hunting for turtle eggs and had a famous fried-egg feast that night.

The entire day the boys pranced about, chased each other round and round, jumped into the river, and splashed water in each other's faces with their palms.

Finally, tired and bored of it all, they lay down on the dry, hot sand. Tom found himself writing 'BECKY' in the sand with his big toe. He was so homesick that he was almost in tears, but tried hard not to show it. He had a secret, which he was not ready to tell, yet.

Huck was melancholy, too. Joe sat poking up the sand with a stick and looking very gloomy.

Finally he said, "Oh, boys, let's give it up. I want to go home. It's so lonesome."

"Oh no, Joe, you'll feel better soon," said Tom. "Just think of the splendid fishing that's here."

"I don't care for fishing. I just want to go home."

"But, Joe, there isn't any swimming place like this anywhere."

"I don't care for it, either. I want to go home."

"Well, we'll let the crybaby go home, won't we, Huck?" said Tom turning to Huck. "You like it here, don't you, Huck?"

Huck said, "Y-e-s"–without any heart in it.

"I'll never speak to you again as long as I live," said Joe, getting up.

And he moved moodily away and began to dress himself.

"Who cares!" said Tom. "Nobody wants you to. Go home and everybody will laugh at you."

Presently, without a parting word, Joe began to wade off toward the Illinois shore. Tom's heart began to sink. He glanced at Huck.

Huck dropped his eyes and said, "Let's us go, too, Tom."

"I won't! You can all go, if you want to. I mean to stay."

Huck began to pick up his scattered clothes. He said, "Tom, I wish you'd come, too. Now you think it over. We'll wait for you when we get to shore."

Huck walked sorrowfully away, and Tom stood looking after him, with a strong desire tugging at his heart to let go his pride and go along too. Finally, he could not take it any more and he darted after his comrades, shouting, "Wait! Wait! I want to tell you something!"

Joe and Huck stopped and turned around. When Tom reached them, he began telling his secret. Joe and Huck listened moodily till at last they saw the point he was driving at. Then they let out a war whoop of applause and said it was splendid!

The lads came gaily back, chattering all the time about Tom's awesome plan and declared that if they had been told earlier about it they wouldn't have wanted to go away!

CHAPTER 8

Returning Home

The Saturday afternoon found the Harpers and Aunt Polly's family in mourning. An unusual quiet spread through the village. The villagers went about their work absentmindedly, talking little and sighing often.

In the afternoon, Becky Thatcher found herself moping about the deserted schoolhouse yard, feeling sad and miserable. But there was nothing to comfort her.

"Oh, if I only had the brass knob again!" she said to herself. "Now I have got nothing to remember him by. He's gone now and I'll never, never see him any more!"

Becky wandered away, with tears rolling down her cheeks.

Nearby, a group of boys and girls—playmates of Tom's and Joe's—stood talking as to how Tom did so-and-so the last time they saw him, and how Joe said this and that.

Then there was a quarrel as to who saw the dead boys last in life, and exchanged the last words with them. All the rest envied the lucky winners. One poor chap, who had no other greatness to offer, said quite proudly, "Well, Tom Sawyer thrashed me once."

But that bid for glory was a failure, for most

of the boys could say that. At last, the group wandered away, still recalling memories of the lost heroes in awed voices.

The next morning, the church bell began to toll and the villagers began to gather, talking in whispers about the sad event. None could remember when the little church had been so full before. Aunt Polly entered, followed by Sid and Mary, and then by the Harper family—all in deep black. The whole parishioners rose respectfully and stood until the mourners were seated in the front pew. Then the minister spread his hands and prayed. A moving hymn was sung, and the text followed, "I am the Resurrection and the Life."

As the service proceeded, the clergyman drew such excellent pictures of the lost lads, and praised their endearing ways so much, that every person in the church felt a pang in his or her heart. They wondered how they could have been so blind to their good qualities before, and had seen only faults and flaws in the poor boys! As the minister related many touching incidents in the lives of the boys, which illustrated their sweet, generous natures, the people became more and more moved. Finally, the whole company broke down crying and the preacher himself gave way to his feelings, and started crying in the pulpit.

There was a rustle in the gallery, which nobody noticed. A moment later, the church door creaked; the minister raised his tear-filled eyes above his handkerchief, and stood transfixed! First one and then another pair of eyes followed the minister's, and then the entire congregation rose and stared while the three dead boys came marching up the aisle—Tom in the lead, Joe next, and Huck at the end!

The boys had been hiding in the unused gallery listening to their own funeral sermon!

Aunt Polly, Mary, and the Harpers threw themselves upon their restored ones, smothering them with kisses. Even Huck was not left out. Aunt

Polly lavished upon him hugs and kisses, making him squirm with embarrassment.

Suddenly, the minister shouted at the top of his voice, "Praise God, from whom all blessings flow, and put your hearts in it!"

And they did. The old church boomed with the singing of a hundred voices. While it shook the rafters, Tom Sawyer looked around and confessed in his heart, that this was the proudest moment of his life.

CHAPTER 9

Tom's Jealousy

That was Tom's great secret—the scheme to return home with his brother pirates, and attend their own funerals. They had paddled over to the Missouri shore on a log, at dusk on Saturday, landing five or six miles below the village. They had slept in the woods at the edge of the town till nearly daylight, and then had crept through back lanes and alleys, and finished their sleep in the gallery of the church.

On Monday morning, during breakfast, Aunt Polly and Mary were very loving to Tom, and very attentive to his wants. There was an unusual amount of talk. In the course of it Aunt Polly said, "Well, I am not saying it wasn't a fine joke, Tom, to keep everybody suffering for almost a week so that you boys could have a good time. But it is a pity you could be as hard-hearted as to let me suffer so. If you could come over to your funeral, you could also have come over and given me a hint that you weren't dead. I wish you cared a little more for me."

"Now, auntie, you know I do care for you," said Tom.

"I'd know it better if you acted more like it."

"I wish now, I had thought," said Tom, thinking quickly. "But I dreamt about you, anyway. That's something, isn't it? Wednesday night I dreamt that you were sitting over there by the bed, and Sid and Mary next to you..."

And then Tom narrated everything he had seen and heard that night. He concluded his tale with these words, "I wrote on a piece of sycamore bark–'we aren't dead, we are only off being pirates.' Then I thought I leaned over and kissed you."

"Did you Tom, did you? I forgive all your mischief for that!"

Aunt Polly seized the boy in a crushing embrace that made him feel like the guiltiest of villains. Aunt Polly was convinced that Tom had some special powers, and that an angel must have been looking over him. She rewarded him with a big, red apple and plenty of kisses before sending him off to school.

At school Tom was a big hero. He did not go skipping and running about as before, but moved with a dignified swagger as suited a proper pirate. Smaller boys followed him about, proud to be

seen with him. Boys his own size were filled with envy. They would have given anything to have Tom's swarthy, suntanned skin, and his glittering status.

The children made so much of him and Joe that the two heroes soon became intolerably 'stuck-up.' They began to tell and retell their adventures to hungry listeners, and their imagination constantly supplied them with new and striking additions.

Tom decided that he could be independent of Becky Thatcher now. Glory was sufficient. He would live for glory! Now that he was famous, maybe she herself would want to 'make up' with him. Well, let her—she should see that he could be as indifferent as some other people.

Presently Becky arrived. Tom pretended not to see her. He moved away, and began talking to a group of boys and girls. Soon, Tom observed that Becky was tripping gaily back and forth with flushed face and dancing eyes, pretending to be busy chasing school mates, and screaming with laughter. However, Tom completely ignored her and continued talking. When Becky observed that Tom was now talking more to Amy Lawrence than to any one else, she felt a sharp pang and grew uneasy at once. She tried to go away, but her feet carried her to the group instead. She said to a girl next to Tom, "Why, Mary Austin! Why didn't you come to Sunday school?"

"I did come—didn't you see me?"

"Did you? Why, it's funny, I didn't see you. I wanted to tell you about the picnic."

"Oh, that's jolly. Who's going to give it?"

"My mother's going to let me have one."

"Oh, won't it be fun! Are you going to invite all the girls and boys?"

"Yes, every one who's my friend—or wants to be," and she glanced slyly at Tom.

But Tom continued talking to Amy Lawrence.

"Oh, may I come?" asked Grace Miller.

"Yes."

"And me?" asked Sally Rogers.

"Yes."

"And me, too?" asked Susy Harper. "And Joe?"

"Yes."

And so on, till the entire group had begged for invitations except Tom and Amy. Then Tom turned coolly away, still talking, and took Amy with him. Becky's lips trembled and tears came to her eyes. But she hid these signs and went on chattering. She got away as soon as she could, hid herself and had a good cry. Then she sat moodily–with wounded pride–and started thinking of a way to get even with Tom.

During recess, Tom continued his flirtation with Amy after ensuring that Becky was witnessing all this. But when Tom saw Becky sitting cozily on a little bench behind the schoolhouse looking at a picture book with Alfred Temple, he got a jolt.

Becky and Alfred seemed so absorbed, and their heads were so close together over the book, that jealousy ran red hot through Tom's veins. He began to hate himself for throwing away the chance Becky had offered for a compromise. He called himself a fool, and all the hard names he could think of. He wanted to cry with vexation.

Finally, when he could tolerate it no more, Tom went home thinking of all sorts of ways to thrash Alfred and teach him a lesson.

Meanwhile, as soon as Becky realized that Tom had gone away, she lost all interest in Alfred. Poor Alfred, seeing that he was losing Becky's attention, kept pointing at the book and exclaiming, "Oh, here's a jolly one! Look at this!"

At last Becky lost her patience, and said, "Oh, don't bother me! I don't care for these pictures!"

And she burst into tears. Alfred was going to try to comfort her, but Becky cried, "Go away and leave me alone! I hate you!"

So the boy halted, wondering what he had done! Alfred went into the deserted schoolhouse, humiliated and angry. Gradually he guessed at the truth—Becky had simply made use of him to make Tom Sawyer jealous.

Alfred now wished there was some way to take revenge on Tom without risking himself. Suddenly he noticed Tom's spelling book had fallen, and realized that here was his opportunity. Alfred opened the lesson for the afternoon and poured ink on the page.

Becky, who at the same moment was glancing in at a window behind him, saw everything. She started homeward, intending to find Tom and tell him what she had seen. Tom would be thankful and their troubles would be healed. Before she was half way home, however, she had changed her mind. She thought of the way Tom had treated her, and was filled with anger. She resolved to let Tom be punished. She also made up her mind to hate Tom forever.

CHAPTER 10

Tom Does A Noble Deed

Tom arrived home in a dreary mood, and the first thing his aunt said to him was, "Tom, I've a notion to skin you alive!"

"Auntie, what have I done?"

"Well, you've done enough. I went to Mrs. Harper—like an old softy—expecting her to believe all the rubbish about that dream you told me about. But Joe had told her everything that had actually happened, and that you had come here and heard all the talk we had that night! Tom, I don't know what is to become of a boy who will act like that. It makes me feel so bad to think you could let me make such a fool of myself before Mrs. Harper, and never say a word."

Tom's smartness of the morning–that had seemed so heroic earlier–merely looked mean and shabby to him now. He hung his head and could not think of anything to say for a moment.

Then he said, "Auntie, I wish I hadn't done it–but I didn't think."

"Oh, child, you never think. You never think of anything but your own selfishness. You could think to come all the way over here from Jackson's Island in the night, to laugh at our troubles and to fool me with a lie about a dream; but you couldn't think to pity us and save us from sorrow."

"Auntie, I know now it was mean, but I didn't

mean to. I didn't, honest. And besides, I didn't come here to laugh at you that night."

"What did you come for, then?"

"It was to tell you not to worry about us, because we hadn't got drowned."

"Tom, Tom, I would be the most thankful person in this world, if I could believe you really thought that! But you know you never did—and I know it, Tom."

"Indeed I did, auntie—I wish I may never stir if I didn't."

"I'd give the whole world to believe that. But it isn't reasonable; because, why didn't you tell me, child?"

"Why, you see, when you started talking about the funeral, I began to think of an idea— of our coming and hiding in the church—and I couldn't somehow bear to spoil it. So I just put the bark back in my pocket."

"What bark?"

"The bark I had wrote on to tell you we'd

gone pirating. I wish now you'd woken up when I kissed you–I do, honest."

The hard lines in his aunt's face relaxed and a sudden tenderness dawned in her eyes.

"Did you kiss me, Tom?"

"Why, yes, I did."

"What did you kiss me for, Tom?"

"Because I loved you so, and you laid there moaning and I was so sorry."

The words sounded like truth. The old lady could not hide a tremble in her voice when she said, "Kiss me again, Tom. Now be off to school and don't bother me any more."

As soon as Tom was gone, Aunt Polly ran to a closet and got out the ruined jacket, which Tom had gone pirating in. Then she muttered to herself, "No, I don't dare. I don't want to find out it's a lie. I won't look."

She put the jacket away, and stood by thinking a minute. Twice she put out her hand to take the garment again, and twice she stopped. Finally, she took out the bark from the pocket and started reading. Soon, tears were flowing from her eyes.

"I could forgive the boy, now," she said, "even if he had committed a million sins!"

There was something in Aunt Polly's manner when she kissed Tom, which made him light-hearted and happy again. He started towards school and had the luck of coming upon Becky Thatcher at the head of Meadow Lane. His mood always determined his manner. So, without a moment's hesitation he ran to her and said, "I was mean today, Becky, and I'm so sorry. I won't ever, ever do something like that again, as long as I live—please make up, won't you?"

The girl stopped and looked him scornfully in the face,

"Mr. Thomas Sawyer, I'll never speak to you again."

She tossed her head and passed on. Tom was so stunned that he did not even have the presence

of mind to say, 'Who cares, Miss Smarty?' until the right time to say it had gone by.

So he said nothing. But he was quite angry, nevertheless. He moped into the schoolyard wishing Becky were a boy, and imagining how he would thrash her if she were. He presently came across her and sent a stinging remark in her direction. Becky too hurled one at him in return. And now she was impatient to see Tom flogged for the spoiled spelling book.

Poor girl, she did not know how fast she was nearing the trouble herself! As Becky was passing by their teacher's desk, which stood near the door, she noticed that the key was in the lock! This drawer contained a book that only the teacher, Mr. Dobbins, was allowed to read. There was not one child in school who was not dying to have a glimpse of it, but the chance never came. So, it was a precious moment for Becky. She glanced around, and the next instant had the book in her hands.

Becky opened the book and discovered that

it was an anatomy textbook that Mr. Dobbins possessed, as his true ambition was to become a doctor. She opened it to the front page, which showed a stark naked figure. At that very moment, Tom entered the room. His entry startled Becky so much that she ripped that page. Then realizing what had happened, she thrust the volume into the desk, turned the key, and burst out crying with shame and vexation.

"Tom Sawyer, you are just as mean as you can be; to sneak up on a person and look at what they're looking at."

"How could I know you were looking at anything?"

"You ought to be ashamed of yourself, Tom Sawyer. You know you're going to tell on me! Oh, what shall I do, what shall I do! I'll be whipped, and I have never ever been whipped in school."

And Becky flung out of the room with an explosion of crying.

The class filed in, and soon the spelling book

discovery was made. For a moment, Becky thought of revealing Alfred's crime, but the next moment when she thought how Tom would soon tell the teacher about her crime, she kept mum.

Tom took his whipping and went back to his seat not at all broken-hearted. He thought he had perhaps unknowingly upset the ink on the spelling book.

A whole hour drifted by, and Mr. Dobbins sat nodding in his chair. By and by, he straightened himself up, yawned, then unlocked his desk, took out his book and settled himself in his chair to read!

Tom shot a glance at Becky. The poor girl had a hunted and helpless rabbit look on her face! Instantly, Tom forgot his quarrel with her. Quick, something must be done! He had to help Becky!

But it was too late to help Becky now. The master faced the students and spoke out in a grave and thundering voice, "Who tore this book?"

There was not a sound. One could have heard a pin drop. The stillness continued; the master searched face after face for signs of guilt.

"Benjamin Rogers, did you tear this book?"

"No sir!"

"Joseph Harper, did you?"

"No sir!"

Mr. Dobbins scanned the rows of boys—considered a while—then turned to the girls. "Amy Lawrence?"

A shake of the head.

"Gracie Miller?"

The same sign.

"Susan Harper, did you do this?"

Another no.

The next girl was Becky Thatcher. Tom was trembling from head to foot with excitement and a sense of the hopelessness of the situation.

"Rebecca Thatcher…"

Tom glanced at Becky's face—it was white with terror.

"…did you tear–no, look me in the face. Did you tear this book?"

A thought shot like lightning through Tom's brain. He sprang to his feet and shouted– "I did it!"

All the children looked surprised at his foolishness, while Tom prepared himself for a second whipping. But as he stepped forward to take his punishment, the surprise, the gratitude, and the adoration that shone upon him from poor Becky's eyes seemed pay enough for a hundred floggings.

Tom and Becky were friends again.

CHAPTER 11.

Justice

It was time for the summer vacations, and Becky Thatcher went to her Constantinople home to stay with her parents during the holidays.

And as if it was not cause enough for Tom to be miserable, he then caught the measles.

During five long weeks, Tom was a prisoner in his house—dead to the world and its happenings.

He was very ill, and was interested in nothing. The time he spent lying in bed seemed an entire age.

When Tom recovered at last, he found that the murder trial had come on in the court. It was the absorbing topic of village talk, and Tom could not get away from it. Every reference to the murder sent a shudder to his heart and his troubled conscience. It kept him in a cold shiver all the time.

At last Tom could bear it no more. He took Huck to a lonely place to have a talk with him.

"Huck, have you ever told anybody about that?"

"About what?"

"You know what."

"Oh—of course I haven't."

"Never a word?"

"Never a solitary word, so help me. Why, Tom Sawyer, we wouldn't remain alive for even two days if that got found out. You know that."

Tom felt more comfortable. After a pause:

"What is the talk around, Huck? I've heard that there is no hope for him. Don't you feel sorry for him, sometimes?"

"Almost always. He hasn't ever done anything to hurt anybody. Just fishes a little to get money to get drunk on, and loiters around. But we all do that. And he's kind of good– he gave me half a fish once, when there wasn't even enough for two."

"Well, he's mended kites for me, Huck, and knitted hooks on to my line. I wish we could get him out of there."

"My! We couldn't get him out, Tom. And besides, it wouldn't do any good; they'd catch him again."

"Yes, and I've heard them say that if he was to get free, they'd lynch him."

"And they'd do it, too."

The boys had a long talk, but it brought them little comfort. As dusk fell, they found themselves hanging about the neighborhood of the little isolated jail.

The boys did as they had often done before—went to the grilled window cell and gave Potter some tobacco and matches. He was on the ground floor and there were no guards.

Muff Potter's gratitude for their gifts cut them deeper than ever this time. The two felt cowardly and treacherous to the last degree when Potter said, "You've been mighty good to me, boys—better than anybody else in this town. Shake hands—yours will come through the bars, but mine's too big. Little hands, and weak—but they've helped Muff Potter a lot, and they'd help him more if they could."

Tom went home miserable, and his dreams that night were full of horrors. Huck was having the same experience. At the end of the second day, the village talk was to the effect that Injun Joe's evidence stood firm and unshaken, and that there was not the slightest question as to what the jury's verdict would be–Muff Potter would be charged! Tom was out late that night, and came to bed through the window. He was in a tremendous state of excitement and it was hours before he got to sleep.

All the village flocked to the court house the next morning, for this was to be the great day. After a long wait, the jury filed in and took their places; shortly afterward, Potter– pale and haggard, timid and hopeless–was brought in, with chains upon him.

Injun Joe was also there, standing emotionless as ever. There was another pause, and then the judge arrived and the sheriff proclaimed the opening of the court.

The counsel for prosecution brought one witness after the other, and soon Muff Potter's crime was proven to be indisputable. More so, as the counsel for defense mysteriously refrained from cross-examining the witnesses!

Finally, the counsel for the prosecution said,

"It is now evident from the oaths of all these responsible citizens, that the crime had been committed by the prisoner at the bar. We rest our case here."

A groan escaped from poor Potter, and he put his face in his hands and rocked his body softly to and fro, while a painful silence reigned in the courtroom. Many men were moved, and many women were in tears.

At last, the counsel for the defense rose and said, "Your honor, I would like to call Thomas Sawyer to the stand!"

Every eye in the court stared with amazed interest at Tom, as he rose and took his place upon the stand. The boy looked wild enough, for he was badly scared. The oath was administered.

"Thomas Sawyer, where were you on the seventeenth of June, at midnight?"

Tom glanced at Injun Joe's iron face and his voice failed him. The audience listened breathlessly, but the words refused to come. After a few moments, however, the boy got a little of his strength back, and managed to say, "In the graveyard!"

"A little bit louder, please. Don't be afraid."

"In the graveyard."

"Now, my boy, tell us everything that occurred–tell it in your own way–don't skip anything, and don't be afraid."

Tom began–hesitatingly at first–but as he warmed to his subject, his words came out more and more easily; in a little while every sound ceased but his own voice; every eye fixed itself upon him. With parted lips and bated breath, the audience hung upon his words, taking no note of time, captivated by the ghastly fascinations of the tale. The pent up emotion reached its climax when the boy said, "–and as the doctor fetched the board around and Muff Potter fell, Injun Joe jumped with the knife and–"

Crash! Quick as lightning, Injun Joe sprang towards a window, broke through the glass, and was gone!

CHAPTER 12

The Treasure Hunt

Muff Potter was released.

The fickle, unreasoning world typically loved and fondled Muff as abundantly as it had ill-treated him before. The poor man was so grateful to Tom, that the boy was quite glad he had spoken the truth. Tom was a hero once more—the pet of the old, the envy of the young. His name even appeared in the village paper.

However, when night fell, Tom wished he had sealed up his tongue. Although his days were of grandeur and jubilation to him, Tom's nights were seasons of horror. Injun Joe infested all his dreams, and always with death in his eye. Hardly any temptation could persuade the boy to stir outdoors after nightfall. Poor Huck was in the same state of wretchedness and terror, for Tom had told the whole story to the lawyer the night before the great day of the trial; and Huck was all the time afraid that his share in the business might leak out.

Half the time Tom was afraid that Injun Joe would never be captured; the other half he was afraid he would be. He felt sure he never could draw a safe breath again until that man was dead and he had seen the corpse.

Rewards had been offered, the country had been searched, but Injun Joe was not found. Tom felt just as insecure as he was before.

However, with time, the murder trial and all the associated events were forgotten, and things returned to normal in the village. Tom and Huck, too, gradually forgot their fears.

Then, one day Tom decided to dig for hidden treasure. Immediately he went looking for Huck Finn to make him his accomplice. Tom took him to a private place and confided the matter to him.

Huck was at once eager and willing.

"Where shall we dig?" asked Huck.

"Oh, anywhere," replied Tom.

"Why, is it hid all around?"

"No, indeed it isn't. It's sometimes hid on islands, sometimes in rotten chests under the roots of an old dead tree; but mostly under the floor in haunted houses."

"Who hides it?"

"Why, robbers, of course."

"Don't they come after it any more?"

"No, they think they will, but they generally forget the marks, or else they die."

"But tell me, where are you going to dig first?"

"Well, I don't know. Suppose we tackle that old dead tree on the hill, the other side of Still-House branch?"

"I agree."

So they got a hold of a broken pick and a shovel, and set out on their three mile trek. They arrived at their destination hot and panting, and threw themselves down in the shade of a neighboring elm to rest.

"I like this," said Tom.

"So do I."

"Say, Huck, if we find a treasure here, what you going to do with your share?"

"Well, I'll have pie and a glass of soda every day, and I'll go to every circus that comes along."

"Aren't you going to save any of it?"

"Save it? What for?"

"To have something to live on in the future."

"But Huck, ghosts won't stop us from digging there in the daytime."

"Well, all right," said Huck, doubtfully. "We'll deal with the haunted house if you say so—but I think it is taking chances."

CHAPTER 13

Coming Across Criminals

When they reached the haunted house, there was something so weird and frightening, and something so depressing about the lonely and desolate place, that the boys were afraid to go in. Then they crept to the door and took a trembling peep. They saw a weed-grown, unplastered floorless room, an ancient fireplace, vacant windows, and a ruinous staircase. Cobwebs grew everywhere over the place.

Tom and Huck entered softly, talking in whispers. Their ears were alert to catch even the slightest sound, and their muscles were tense and ready for instant retreat.

In a little while, however, their fears had lessened and they gave the place a critical and interested examination. Next they threw their tools into a corner and went to have a look upstairs. There, in one corner they found a closet that promised mystery; but the promise was a fraud—there was nothing in it. The boys' courage had grown quite strong now. They were about to go down and begin work when…

"Sh!" said Tom.

"What is it?" whispered Huck, going pale with fright.

"Sh! There! … Hear it?"

"Yes! … Oh, my! Let's run!"

"Keep still! Don't you move! They're coming right toward the door."

The boys stretched themselves upon the floor with their eyes to the knotholes in the rotting planking, and lay waiting in misery and fear.

"They've stopped–no–they're coming–here they are. Don't whisper another word, Huck. My goodness, I wish I was out of this!"

Two men entered. Each boy thought, 'There's the old deaf and dumb beggar that's been about town once or twice lately, but never seen the other man before.'

The 'other' was a ragged, unkempt creature, with an unpleasant face. The beggar was wrapped in a shawl; he had bushy white whiskers; long white hair flowed from under his broad-brimmed hat, and he wore green goggles.

"No," the unpleasant-faced man was saying, "I've thought it all over, and I don't like it. It's dangerous."

"Dangerous!" grunted the 'deaf and dumb'

beggar, to the immense surprise of the boys. "Milksop!"

This voice made the boys gasp and quake. It was Injun Joe's! There was silence for some time.

Then Joe said, "What's more dangerous than coming here in the daytime? Anybody who saw us would be suspicious!"

"I know that. But there wasn't any other place as handy. I want to quit this shanty—and I wanted to yesterday—only it wasn't possible with those infernal boys playing over there on the hill, right in full view."

Meanwhile, 'those infernal boys' above heard this remark and shuddered.

The two men got out some food and had lunch. Soon, they started yawning and the next moment fell fast asleep.

The boys drew a long, grateful breath. Tom whispered, "Now's our chance—come!"

Huck said, "I can't. I'd die if they awoke."

Although Tom urged him again and again, Huck held back. At last Tom slowly got up, and started alone. But his very first step caused such a hideous creak from the crazy floor that he sank down almost dead with fright. He never made a second attempt.

After a long and seemingly endless waiting, Injun Joe woke up. He sat up, stared around, smiled grimly upon his comrade whose head was drooping upon his knees, stirred him up with his foot and said, "Here! Get up! You're a watchman, aren't you?"

"My! Have I been asleep?"

"Yes, it's now time for us to be moving, partner. But what'll we do with that?"

"I think we should leave it here as we've always done. Six hundred and fifty in silver's too much to carry."

"All right; but to be safe we'll just bury it deep."

Injun Joe's partner walked across the room,

knelt down, raised one of the hearthstones and took out a bag that jingled. He then passed the bag to Injun Joe, who was on his knees in the corner, digging with his knife.

The boys forgot all their fears and miseries in an instant. With gloating eyes they watched every movement. Six hundred and fifty pieces of silver were enough to make half a dozen boys rich! Here was treasure being buried under their very noses! There would not be any bothersome uncertainty now as to where to dig. The boys nudged each other every moment, which simply meant—"Oh, aren't you glad now we're here!"

At this moment, Joe's knife struck upon something.

"Hello!" said he.

"What is it?" asked his comrade.

"Half-rotten box, I believe."

He reached his hand in and drew out some of its contents.

"Man, it's money!" he exclaimed.

The two men examined the handful of coins. These were gold coins. The boys above were as excited as the two men, and as delighted.

Joe's comrade said, "There's an old rusty pick amongst the weeds in the corner—I saw it a minute ago."

He ran and brought the boys' pick and shovel. Injun Joe took the pick, looked it over critically, shook his head, muttered something, and then began to use it. The box was soon unearthed. It was an old and rusty iron box.

"Partner, there are thousands of dollars here!" cried Injun Joe, his eyes shining brightly.

"This must be the place where Murrel's gang buried their loot," the other man observed.

"I know it," said Injun Joe; "and this looks like it, I should say."

"Now you won't need to do that job."

Injun Joe frowned.

"You don't know me," he almost hissed. "It isn't robbery altogether, it's revenge!" and a wicked light flamed in his eyes. "I'll need your help in it. When it's finished, you can go home to your Nance and your kids."

"Well, what'll we do with this; bury it again?"

"Yes."

Overhead, two pair of ears pricked delightedly.

"No! Wait a moment; the pick and shovel had fresh earth on them!"

Instantly, the two boys upstairs turned sick with terror.

Injun Joe, meanwhile, continued, "What business has a pick and a shovel here? Someone must have brought them, and they must be somewhere around! And if we just bury it again the person or persons will surely come and see the ground disturbed! No! We'll take the box to my den."

"Why, of course!" exclaimed the other man. "I should have thought of that before. You mean Number one?"

"No - Number two - under the cross. The other place is too common."

"All right, let's start then. It's nearly dark."

Shortly afterward, the two men slipped out of the house in the deepening dusk, and moved toward the river with their precious box.

Tom and Huck rose up, weak but greatly relieved, and stared after the two through the chinks between the logs of the house. Only when the robbers were completely out of sight did the two dare to come out of the house and start towards the town, absorbed in deep thought.

CHAPTER 14

On The Trail

The adventure of the day greatly tormented Tom's dreams that night. In the morning he had a hurried breakfast and went off to find Huck. Huck was sitting on the riverbank, listlessly dangling his feet in the water and looking very melancholy.

"Hello, Huck!" greeted Tom.

"Hello, yourself."

There was a silence for a minute.

Then Huck spoke up, "Tom, I've had dreams all night, with that patch-eyed devil coming for me - rot him!"

"No, not rot him. Find him!" cried Tom. "We have to track the money! And for that we have to track him out to his 'Number Two'."

"Number Two! Yes, that's it. I have been thinking about that. But I can't make anything out of it. What do you think it is?"

"I don't know; maybe it's the number of a house!"

"No, Tom, the houses don't have any numbers in this town."

"Well, then, let me think a minute. Then it may be the number of a room - in a tavern, you know!"

"That's right! There are only two taverns here! We can find out quick."

"You stay here, Huck, till I come."

Tom was off at once towards the town. He found that in the best tavern, No. 2 had long been occupied by a young lawyer, and was still occupied by him. In the second tavern, the more modest one, No. 2 was a mystery. The tavern-keeper's young son said it was kept locked all the time, and he never saw anybody go into it or come out of it, except at night.

Tom returned to Huck and reported everything.

"That's what I've found out, Huck. I think that's the very No. 2 we're after."

"Now what you going to do, Tom?" asked Huck.

"Let me think."

Tom thought a long time. Then he said, "I'll tell you. The back door of that No. 2 comes out into a little close alley between the tavern and an old brick store. Now you get hold of all the door-keys you can find, and I'll pinch all Aunt Polly's keys, and then we'll go there and try to open the door with them. And mind you, keep a lookout for Injun Joe, because he said he was going to drop into town for a chance to get his revenge. If you see him, just follow him. If he doesn't go to that No. 2, that isn't the place."

That night, Tom and Huck were ready for their adventure. They hung about the neighborhood of the tavern until after nine; one watched the alley, and the other the tavern door. Nobody entered the alley or left it; nobody entered or left the tavern door. After a while, Tom went home, and then around twelve at night, Huck too closed his watch and retired to bed in an empty sugar hogshead.

The boys had the same bad luck on Tuesday and Wednesday. On Thursday night, Tom slipped out with his aunt's old tin lantern and a large towel to blindfold it with. He hid the lantern in Huck's sugar hogshead, and the watch began. An hour before midnight, the tavern closed up and its lights were put out.

The place was now in complete darkness.

Tom got his lantern, lit it in the hogshead, and wrapped it closely in the towel. Then he felt his way into the alley toward the tavern, while Huck stood on guard and waited.

Time elapsed, and Huck started getting anxious. In his uneasiness, Huck found himself drawing closer and closer to the alley, fearing all sorts of dreadful things. Suddenly, there was a flash of light and Tom came running by.

"Run!" said he; "run, for your life!"

Tom needn't have repeated it; once was enough. Huck was already running at a speed of thirty or forty miles an hour. The boys never stopped till they reached an old and abandoned house at the lower end of the village. Just as they got within its shelter, it started raining.

As soon as Tom got his breath, he said, "Huck, it was awful! I tried two of the keys, but they wouldn't turn in the lock. Then without noticing what I was doing, I took hold of the knob, and the door came open! It wasn't locked! I hopped in, and shook off the towel, and, great Caesar's ghost!"

"What! – what did you see, Tom?" cried Huck.

"Huck, I almost stepped onto Injun Joe's hand!"

"No!"

"Yes! He was lying sound asleep on the floor, with his old patch on his eye and his arms spread out."

"Lordy, what did you do? Did he wake up?"

"No, he didn't move. He was drunk, I think."

"Say, Tom, did you see that box?"

"I didn't wait to look around. I didn't see the box, I didn't see the cross. I didn't see anything but a bottle and a tin cup on the floor next to Injun Joe. And yes, I saw two barrels and lots of bottles in the room."

Tom thought for a long time, then he said, "Look here, Huck, let's not try that thing till we know Injun Joe's not in there. It's too scary. We'll keep watch every night, and when we see Injun Joe leave the tavern, then we can go in and take that box.

"I agree," replied Huck. "I'll keep watch every night if you'll do the other part of the job."

"All right, I will. I'll go home now. It'll be daylight soon. You go back and watch that long, will you?"

"I said I would, Tom, and I will. I'll sleep all day and I'll stand watch all night."

"Well, if you see something's up at night, just come to my window and meow," said Tom Sawyer.

CHAPTER 15

Huck Saves Widow Douglas

 riday morning brought good news for Tom -
Judge Thatcher's family had come back to town
the night before. Immediately, both Injun Joe and
the treasure sank into secondary importance, and
Becky took the chief place in Tom's interest. Becky
had got her mother's consent to have the long-
promised and long-delayed picnic the very next

day, and she was delighted. The invitations were sent out before sunset, and directly, the children of the village were thrown into a fever of pleasant anticipation. Tom's excitement enabled him to keep awake until a pretty late hour; moreover, he hoped to hear Huck's 'meow'.

But he was disappointed. No signal came that night.

By ten o'clock in the morning, an excited group of children had gathered at Judge Thatcher's house. Everything was ready for a start, and the old steam ferry-boat was chartered for the occasion. Sid, however, was sick and had to miss the fun, and Mary remained at home to entertain him.

Three miles below town, the ferryboat stopped at the mouth of a woody hollow. The crowd swarmed ashore, and soon the place echoed with shouting and laughter. Soon after, a sumptuous feast was spread, followed by a refreshing period of rest and chat in the shade of spreading oaks. By-and-by somebody shouted, "Who's ready for the cave?"

Everybody was. Bundles of candles were obtained, and straightway there was a general dash up the hill. The mouth of the cave was up the hillside, an opening shaped like the letter A. Inside was a small chamber, chilly as an icehouse, and walled by Nature with solid limestone.

Before long, the procession went down the steep descent of the main avenue. This main avenue was not more than eight or ten feet wide. Every few steps other narrow crevices branched from it on either side - for McDougal's cave was like an enormous maze of twisted passages that ran into each other, and out again, and led nowhere. It was said that one might wander days and nights through its complex tangle of rifts and chasms, and still never find the end of the cave.

The procession moved along the main avenue, and then groups began to slip aside into branch avenues, roam or run along the dismal corridors, and take each other by surprise at points where the corridors joined again.

Time flew by and soon the groups were astonished to find that night was almost approaching. The clanging bell had been calling for half an hour. Soon, the ferryboat with her still excited passengers pushed into the stream.

Huck was already on his watch when the ferry-boat's lights went glinting past the dock. The night was growing cloudy and dark. Ten o'clock came and the noise of vehicles ceased, scattered lights began to wink out, leaving the small watcher alone with the silence and the ghosts.

Eleven o'clock came, and the tavern lights were put out. Huck waited for what seemed to him a long, long time, but nothing happened. His faith was weakening. Was there any use? Why not give it up?

Suddenly there was a noise. The alley door closed softly. Instantly, Huck had sprung to the corner of the brick store. The next moment two men brushed by him, and one seemed to have something under his arm.

'It must be that box!' thought Huck.

Deciding to follow them, Huck stepped out and glided along behind the men, cat-like, with bare feet.

The men moved up the river and then went straight ahead, until they came to the path that led up Cardiff Hill. This they took. Huck followed them as closely as he could, at the same time keeping himself out of their sight. Then, after some time, Huck slackened his pace, fearing he was gaining too fast, and looked around. Then he stopped altogether. He knew he was within five steps of the stile leading into Widow Douglas' grounds. Very well, he thought, let them bury it there; it won't be hard to find.

Now there was a voice - a very low voice – Injun Joe's!

"Maybe she's got company," he was saying. "There are lights!"

"I can't see any."

This was that stranger's voice – the stranger of the haunted house – Injun Joe's comrade! A deadly chill went to Huck's heart - this, then, was the 'revenge' job!

Huck's first impulse was to run away. Then he remembered that the Widow Douglas had been kind to him more than once, and maybe these men were going to murder her. He should warn her!

At this very moment, Injun Joe's companion spoke up.

"Yes. Well, there is company there, I think. Better give it up."

"Give it up? Never! I've told you before, and I'll tell you again. Her husband was the judge who sent me to prison, and before I could take my revenge he died. But I'll take it out on his wife!"

"Oh, don't kill her! Don't do that!"

"Keep your opinion to yourself! It will be safest for you."

Huck held his breath and stepped cautiously

back till he was out of hearing distance. Then he turned in his tracks, turned himself as carefully as if he were a ship - and then walked quickly but carefully along. Finally, when he had put quite a distance between himself and the men, he picked up speed and ran. Down, down he sped, till he reached the Welshman's house, down the hill.

Huck banged frantically at the door, and presently the old man and his two brawny sons looked out of the windows.

Huck explained everything as briefly as he could, and three minutes later the old man and his sons, well armed, were up the hill. Huck hid behind a great boulder and tried to listen.

There was a moment of anxious silence, and then all of a sudden there was an explosion of firearms and a cry.

Huck waited for no details. He sprang away and sped down the hill as fast as his legs could carry him.

CHAPTER 16

An Unfortunate Occurrence

Huck passed a sleepless and anxious night, and as soon as it was daylight, he went back to the Welshman's house, and knocked at the door. He was immediately warmly welcomed inside the house by the Welshman and invited to breakfast.

"Well, my boy," said the Welshman. "I and the boys hoped you'd turn up and stop here last night."

"I was awfully scared," said Huck, "and so I ran away. But I wanted to know what happened and that's why I came here as soon as daylight broke."

"Well, poor chap, you do look as if you've had a hard night! But there's a bed here for you when you've had your breakfast."

Then the Welshman, Mr. Jones narrated to Huck all that took place the previous night. He and his sons had hidden behind the bushes and were only fifteen feet away from Injun Joe, when, unfortunately, a sneeze came upon Mr. Jones!

The robbers became alert and took to their heels. And although Mr. Jones and his sons fired after them, and pursued Injun Joe and his partner for quite some distance, the robbers managed to escape.

Soon, the news of the thrilling incident spread

throughout the village. People discussed the event, and the fact that not a sign of the two villains had been yet discovered. After church, that day, Judge Thatcher's wife walked together with Mrs. Harper down the aisle, and said, "Is my Becky going to sleep all day? I expect she is extremely tired."

"Becky?"

"Why," cried Mrs. Thatcher, with a startled look, "didn't she stay with you last night?"

"Why, no!"

Mrs. Thatcher turned pale and swayed a little, just as Aunt Polly was passing by.

Aunt Polly said, "Good-morning, Mrs. Thatcher; good-morning, Mrs. Harper. I suppose my Tom stayed with one of you last night."

Mrs. Thatcher shook her head feebly and turned paler than ever.

"He didn't stay with us," said Mrs. Harper, beginning to look uneasy.

Anxiety came into Aunt Polly's face.

"Joe Harper, have you seen my Tom this morning?"

"No madam."

"When did you see him last?"

Joe tried to remember, but was not sure. Meanwhile, the people had stopped moving out of church. Whispers passed along, and an uneasy expression appeared on every face. Children were anxiously questioned, but all said they had not noticed whether Tom and Becky were on the ferryboat during the homeward trip. It was dark, and no one thought of inquiring if any one was missing. Finally, one young man blurted out his fear that they were still in the cave!

Mrs. Thatcher swooned away, while Aunt Polly began crying and wringing her hands.

The alarm swept from lip to lip, from group to group, from street to street, and within five minutes the bells were wildly sounding and the whole town was up! Horses were saddled, the ferryboat ordered out, and within half an hour, two hundred men were pouring down the highroad and river toward the cave.

In the meantime Huck was delirious with fever. He was still in the house of Mr. Jones. The doctors were all at the cave, so the Widow Douglas came and took charge of the patient. She said she would do her best for Huck. And indeed, she looked after him day and night, till, after three days, Huck gained consciousness. He feebly led up to the subject of taverns, and finally asked if anything had been discovered at the Temperance Tavern since he had been ill.

"Yes," said the Widow.

Huck sat up in bed, wild-eyed.

"What? What was it?"

"Liquor! The owner of the place kept liquors illegally, and the place has been shut up. Now lie down, child, what a fright you did give me!"

"Only tell me just one thing please! Was it Tom Sawyer that found it?"

The widow burst into tears.

"Hush, hush, child, hush! I've told you before, you must not talk. You are very, very sick!"

Huck obeyed, thinking to himself, 'So the treasure was gone forever! But what was the Widow crying about? That was curious!' And soon he fell asleep.

'He's asleep, poor child,' thought the widow. 'Did Tom Sawyer find it! Only if somebody could find Tom Sawyer! Ah, there aren't many who are hopeful now, or have enough strength left to go on searching.'

People had been searching for Tom and Becky for three days now. And though many things belonging to the children had been found, the two were still missing. And the hope to find the two was diminishing fast.

CHAPTER 17

Lost In The Cave

Tom and Becky had tripped along the dark passageways with the rest of the children, visiting the familiar wonders of the cave. In a while the hide-and-seek play began, and Tom and Becky enthusiastically participated in it, until they were quite tired. Then they wandered down a winding path, holding up their candles and reading the tangled web-work of names, dates, and mottoes inscribed on the rocky walls. Still drifting along and talking, they scarcely noticed that they were now in a part of the cave whose walls were not inscribed.

In a while they had gone far down into the secret depths of the cave, and came to spring in the middle of a cavern whose walls were supported by many fantastic pillars. These pillars had been formed by the joining of great stalactites and stalagmites. Under their roof, thousands of bats had packed themselves. The lights carried by the children disturbed the creatures, and they came flocking down, squeaking and darting furiously at the candles.

Tom quickly seized Becky's hand and hurried her into the first corridor that he saw. The bats chased the children a good distance; but they plunged into every new passage that came up, and at last got rid of the terrifying creatures.

At last, the exhausted children sat down by a lake and rested. Now, for the first time, the deep stillness of the place got a hold upon the spirits of the children. Becky said, "It's long since I heard any of the others. I wonder how long we've been down here, Tom. We better start back."

Tom agreed, and they walked in silence through a corridor for a long distance, glancing at each new opening, to see if it looked familiar; but they were all strange.

After a while Tom started feeling less and less hopeful.

"Becky, I was such a fool!" he cried. "I never thought we might want to come back! Now I can't find the way. It's all mixed up."

"Tom, Tom, we're lost! We never can get out of this awful place! Oh, why did we ever leave the others?"

Becky sank to the ground and burst out crying. Tom sat down next to her, put his arms around her, and begged her to pluck up hope again. In a while, Becky calmed down and they moved on again, aimlessly, for all they could do was to keep moving.

By-and-by Tom took Becky's candle and blew it out. Becky understood. She knew that although Tom had another whole candle in his pocket, yet he must economize. The children, fatigued after their long walk, soon drowsed off to sleep.

When they awoke, Tom lighted a candle, and the two wandered along again, hand in hand. Then Tom said they must try to listen for dripping water - they must find a spring. They found one presently, and Tom said it was time to rest again. They sat down, and Becky declared she was hungry.

Tom took a piece of cake out of his pocket which he had saved from the picnic, and divided it between them. The children ate and drank the refreshing water from the spring. Then Becky suggested that they should move on again. Tom was silent for a moment. Then he revealed that the lighted candle was their last one!

The distressed children fastened their eyes upon their bit of candle and watched it melt slowly and pitilessly away; till at last a feeble flame rose and fell, and died out completely. The horror of utter darkness ruled now!

The two tried to console each other. Tom said that they must have been missed long ago, and no doubt the search was going on. But when he shouted out, only terrifying echoes came back to him.

The hours wasted away, and hunger came to torment the captives again. A portion of Tom's half of the cake was left; they divided and ate it. But they seemed hungrier than before.

By-and-by Tom said, "Sh! Did you hear that?"

Both held their breath and listened. There was a faint sound. Instantly, Tom answered it, and leading Becky by the hand, started groping down the corridor in its direction. Presently, the sound was heard again, a little nearer this time.

"It's them!" said Tom; "they're coming! Come along, Becky, we'll be saved now!"

The joy of the prisoners was almost overwhelming. Tom went ahead and reached a jutting, cliff-like projection in the cave. He looked down. At that very moment, not twenty yards away, a human hand, holding a candle, appeared from behind a rock! Tom shouted, and the next moment, the hand was followed by the body it belonged to - Injun Joe's!

Tom was paralyzed; he could not move. But he was greatly relieved to see the robber take to his heels and get out of sight. Tom wondered why Joe had not recognized his voice and come over and killed him for testifying in court. Then he reasoned that the echoes must have disguised the voice. Tom's fright weakened every muscle in his body. However, hunger and dejection rose above their fears in the long run.

After another long sleep, the children awoke tortured with a raging hunger. Tom believed that it must be Wednesday or Thursday or even Friday or Saturday, now, and that the search had been given over. He proposed to explore another passage. But Becky was very weak and said she would remain where she was, and die.

Tom kissed her, with a choking sensation in his throat, and told her that he would surely find the searchers or an escape from the cave. Then leaving her behind, he went groping down one of the passages on his hands and knees, distressed with hunger and sick with bodings of coming doom.

CHAPTER 18

Escape!

In the middle of Tuesday night, a wild ringing burst from the village bells. Within a few moments, the streets were swarming with frantic people, who shouted, "They're found! They're found!"

The crowd moved toward the river, met Tom and Becky coming in an open carriage drawn by shouting citizens, joined its homeward march, and swept up the main street roaring hurrah after hurrah!

The village was lighted up; nobody went to bed again. It was the greatest night the little town had ever seen. A procession of villagers filed through Judge Thatcher's house, seized the saved ones and kissed them, squeezed Mrs. Thatcher's hand, and drifted out, raining tears all over the place.

Aunt Polly's happiness was complete. A messenger was sent with the news of the rescue to Judge Thatcher who was still at the cave, searching for the children.

Tom lay upon a sofa and narrated his wonderful adventure to the eager audience who had crowded around him, adding many imaginary exploits to it. He closed with a description of how he left Becky, and went on an exploring expedition with the help of his kite lines to prevent getting confused; how he followed two avenues as far as his kite-line would reach; how he followed a third to the fullest stretch of the kite-line, and was about to turn back when he glimpsed a far off speck that looked like daylight. He then dropped the line and fumbled toward it, pushed his head and shoulders through a small hole, and saw the river Mississippi rolling by!

Then he went back for Becky and together they pushed their way out of the hole. Soon, some men came along in a boat and they were saved.

Before dawn, Judge Thatcher and the handful of searchers with him were tracked out in the cave, and informed of the great news.

Tom and Becky were bedridden throughout Wednesday and Thursday. By Friday, Tom was back to his business as usual. Tom learned of Huck's sickness and went to see him, but was warned to keep silent about his adventure and introduce no exciting topic. The Widow Douglas stayed by to see that he obeyed.

At home, Tom learned of the Cardiff Hill event. He also learnt that the body of Injun Joe's companion had eventually been found in the river; he had been drowned while trying to escape.

The next day, Tom went to Judge Thatcher's house to see Becky.

The Judge told him, "Tom, we have taken care that nobody will get lost in that cave any more."

"How?" asked Tom.

"I had its big door sealed two weeks ago, and triple-locked."

Tom turned as white as a sheet.

"What's the matter? Here, run, somebody! Fetch a glass of water!"

The water was brought and thrown into Tom's face.

"What was the matter with you, Tom?"

"Injun Joe's in the cave!"

** ** ** ** ** ** ** ** **

Within a few minutes scores of men were on their way to McDougal's cave. When the cave door was unlocked, a sorrowful sight presented itself in the dim twilight of the place. Injun Joe lay stretched upon the ground, dead. His face was close to the crack of the door, as if his longing eyes had been fixed, to the last moment, upon the light and the cheer of the free world outside.

Tom was touched, for he knew by his own experience how this wretch had suffered. He was full of pity for the dead man, but nevertheless he felt a great sense of relief and security now.

Injun Joe's bowie-knife lay close by, its blade broken in two. The great foundation-beam of the door had been chipped and hacked through, with tedious effort. However it was clearly useless, for a solid rock formed a sill outside the door, and the knife had produced no effect on it; the only damage done was to the knife itself. Ordinarily one could find plenty of candles stuck around in the crevices of the cave, left there by tourists; but there were none now. The prisoner had eaten them. He had also managed to catch a few bats, and these, also he had eaten. The poor unfortunate had starved to death.

Injun Joe was buried near the mouth of the cave.

The morning after the funeral, Tom took Huck to a private place to have an important talk. Huck had learned all about Tom's adventure from Mr. Jones and the Widow Douglas, and now he wanted to tell Tom all about his adventures on Cardiff Hill.

He narrated to his friend how he followed Injun Joe to the Widow Douglas' house.

"You followed him?" asked Tom, surprised.

"Yes – but please don't talk about it. I think Injun Joe has left friends behind him, and I don't want them to take revenge on me."

Then Huck told his entire adventure in confidence to Tom, who had only heard Mr. Jones' part of it before.

"Well," said Huck, coming back to the main question, "whoever pinched the liquor in No. 2 pinched the money too."

"Huck, that money wasn't ever in No. 2! It's in the cave!" said Tom.

Huck's eyes blazed.

"Say the truth, now - is this a joke, Tom, or are you earnest?"

"I am just as earnest as ever I was in my life, Huck. Will you go in there with me and help get it out?"

"You bet I will! When do we start?

"Right now, if you say so. Are you strong enough?"

"Is it far in the cave? I don't think I can walk more than a mile."

"Don't worry. There's a short cut that nobody except me knows about. All we want is some bread and meat, a small bag or two, and two or three kite-strings, and some matches."

So, in the afternoon, the boys borrowed a

small boat and started on their expedition. After a while, their boat neared the opening that Tom and Becky had escaped from.

"Now you see this bluff?" said Tom, pointing high up the hillside. "It looks all alike. But do you see that white place up there? Well, that's one of my marks. We'll get ashore, now."

They landed, and went uphill.

"Huck, now we're standing just near the hole," said Tom. "See if you can find it."

Huck searched the entire place, but found nothing. Then Tom proudly marched into a thick clump of bushes and said, "Here you are! Look at it, Huck; it's the snuggest hole in this country."

The boys then entered through the small opening, Tom in the lead. They worked their way to the farther end of the tunnel, then tied their kite-strings and moved on. A few steps brought them to the spring, and Tom felt a shudder pass all through him. He showed Huck the bit of candlewick perched on a lump of clay against the wall, and described how he and Becky had watched the flame die.

In a while they entered and followed Tom's other corridor until they reached the jutting projection.

Tom whispered, "Now I'll show you something, Huck."

He held up his candle and said, "Do you see that corner? There, on the big rock over there, marked with candle-smoke?"

"Tom, it's a cross!"

"Now, where's your Number Two? 'Under the cross,' right? I saw Injun Joe poke up his candle right there, Huck!"

Huck stared at the cross for a moment, and then said with a shaky voice, "Tom, let's get out of here!"

"What! And leave the treasure?"

"Yes - leave it. Injun Joe's ghost is certainly around there."

Tom tried to convince Huck that there were no ghosts in the cave, but in vain.

At last he said, "Look here, Huck, Injun Joe's ghost isn't a-going to come around where there's a cross!"

That seemed logical, and Huck calmed down. The boys started hunting for the treasure box. Tom moved down first. Huck followed. Four paths opened out of the small cavern in which the great rock stood. The boys examined three of them with no result. In the cavern nearest the base of the rock, they found a small recess with a blanket, an old suspender, some bacon rind, and some well-gnawed chicken bones. But there was no money-box.

Tom said, "He said under the cross. Well, this comes nearest to being under the cross. It can't be under the rock itself, because that sets firm on the ground."

They searched everywhere once more, and then sat down discouraged. Huck could suggest nothing. By-and-by Tom said, "Look here, Huck, there are footprints and some candle-grease on the clay on one side of this rock, but not on the other sides. Now, what's that for? I bet the money is under the rock. I'm going to dig in the clay."

"That isn't a bad idea, Tom!" said Huck with animation.

Tom started digging. He had not dug four inches before he struck wood.

"Huck, do you hear that?"

Huck began to dig and scratch now. Some boards were soon uncovered and removed. They had concealed a natural passage which led under the rock. Tom got into this and followed the winding course of the passage, with Huck at his heels.

By-and-by, Tom turned a short curve and exclaimed, "My goodness, Huck, look here!"

It was the treasure-box, sure enough!

"Got it at last!" said Huck, scooping out the

tarnished, yellow coins with his hand. "We're rich, Tom!"

"Huck, I always thought we'd get it. It's just too good to believe, but we have got it! Let's take it out now."

The money was soon in the bags the boys had brought with them. They presently emerged into the clump of bushes, and looked cautiously out. Finding the coast clear, they sat down in their boat and had lunch.

As the sun dipped toward the horizon, they pushed out their boat into the river. They landed shortly after dark.

"Now, Huck," said Tom, "we'll hide the money in the loft of the Widow's woodshed. I'll come up in the morning and we'll count and divide it, and then we'll hunt up a place in the woods for it, where it will be safe. For now, you just lay quietly here and watch the stuff, while I run and bring Benny Taylor's little wagon. It won't take me long."

He disappeared, and soon returned with the wagon, put the two small sacks into it, threw some old rags on top of them, and started off, dragging his cargo behind him. When the boys reached Mr. Jones' house, they stopped to rest. Just as they were about to move on, the Welshman stepped out and said, "Hello, who's that?"

"Huck and Tom Sawyer."

"Good! Come inside boys, everybody is waiting for you. I'll pull the wagon for you. Why, it's a bit heavy! Got bricks in it or old metal?"

"Old metal," said Tom.

Shortly, Tom and Huck went into Mrs. Douglas' drawing-room. Mr. Jones left the wagon near the door and followed.

The place was grandly lighted, and all important people in the village were there: the Thatchers, the Harpers, the Rogers, Aunt Polly, Sid, Mary, the minister, the editor, and a great many more, and all dressed in their best. The Widow welcomed the boys as heartily as one could welcome such dirty looking creatures who were covered with mud and grease. Aunt Polly blushed crimson with humiliation and frowned and shook her head at Tom.

However, before she could say anything to Tom, Mr. Jones spoke up, "I stumbled on Tom and Huck right at my door, and so I just brought them along in a hurry."

"And you did just right," said the Widow. "Come with me, boys."

She took them to a bedroom and said, "Now wash and dress yourselves. Here are two new suits of clothes - shirts, socks, and everything that you'll need. They'll fit both of you. We'll wait - come down when you are ready."

Then she left.

CHAPTER 19

Tom And Huck Are Rich!

Huck said, "Tom, if we can find a rope, we can climb down. The window isn't high from the ground."

"Why do you want to climb down?" asked Tom.

"Well, I am not used to that kind of a crowd. I can't stand it. I am not going down there, Tom."

"Oh, bother! It isn't anything. I'll take care of you."

Sid appeared.

"Tom," said he, "auntie has been waiting for you all the afternoon. Mary got your Sunday clothes ready, and everybody's been fussing about you. Hello, isn't this grease and mud on your clothes?"

"Now, Mr. Sid, you just mind your own business. What's all this fuss about, anyway?"

"The Widow is giving a party for the Welshman and his sons, on account of that scrape they helped her out of the other night. And I overheard Mr. Jones tell auntie that he was going to announce some secret."

Sid chuckled in a very contented and satisfied way.

Some minutes later, the widow's guests were at the supper-table, and a dozen children were propped up at little side-tables in the same room. After supper, Mr. Jones made his little speech.

He thanked the widow for the honor she was doing himself and his sons, but said that there was another person who was actually responsible for saving the Widow's life, but was too modest to let his name be taken in this regard.

Then he sprung his secret about Huck's share in the adventure in the finest dramatic manner he could. Everyone applauded and complimented Huck, and the Widow heaped so many compliments and so much gratitude upon Huck that he almost forgot the discomfort of his new clothes.

The Widow said she meant to give Huck a home under her roof and have him educated. She also said that when she could spare the money, she would start him in business in a modest way. Now Tom's chance had come.

He said, "Huck doesn't need it. Huck's rich!"

Nothing but a regard for the Widow kept back the people from laughing noisily at this pleasant joke. But the silence was a little awkward. Tom broke it.

"Huck's got money," he declared. "Maybe you don't believe it, but he's got lots of it. Oh, you needn't smile. I think I can show you. Just wait a minute."

Tom ran out of doors. The company looked at each other with a puzzled interest - and inquiringly at Huck, who was tongue-tied.

"Sid, what's wrong with Tom?" said Aunt Polly. "This boy always …"

Tom entered, struggling with the weight of his sacks, and Aunt Polly could not finish her sentence. Tom poured the mass of yellow coins upon the table and said, "There, what did I tell you? Half of it's Huck's and half of it's mine!"

The spectacle took everyone's breath away! All gazed, nobody spoke for a moment. Then there was a unanimous demand for an explanation.

Tom started narrating his story. The tale was long, but interesting, and nobody interrupted Tom in between. When he had finished, Mr. Jones said, "I thought I had a little surprise for this occasion, but now all this makes my surprise amount to nothing!"

The money was counted. The sum amounted to a little over twelve thousand dollars! It was more than any one present had ever seen at one time before.

Tom's and Huck's windfall caused a mighty stir in the poor little village of St. Petersburg. It was talked about, gloated over, and glorified. Wherever Tom and Huck appeared, they were stared at and admired. The village paper published biographical sketches of the boys.

The Widow Douglas put Huck's money in the bank for him, at an interest of six per cent. Judge Thatcher did the same with Tom's money at Aunt Polly's request. Each lad had an income, now, that was simply phenomenal - a dollar a day, each day of the week, and half a dollar on Sundays.

Judge Thatcher had formed a great opinion

of Tom. He said that no ordinary boy would ever have got his daughter out of the cave. When Becky told her father, in strict confidence, how Tom had taken her whipping at school, the Judge was greatly moved. He hoped to see Tom become a great lawyer or a great soldier some day, and said he meant to look to it that Tom should be admitted to the National Military Academy and afterward trained in the best law school in the country, so that he might be ready for either career or both.

Huck Finn's wealth, and the fact that he was now under the Widow Douglas' protection, introduced him to society. Actually, Huck was dragged into it, and his suffering was almost more than he could bear. The widow's servants kept him clean and neat, combed and brushed him. He had to eat with a knife and fork, and to use napkin, cup, and plate. He had to learn his book, he had to go to church, and he had to talk properly. Wherever he turned, the chains and bars of civilization shut him in and bound him hand and foot.

He bravely bore his miseries for three weeks, and then one day he ran away.

For forty-eight hours the widow hunted for him everywhere, in great distress. The public were deeply concerned; they searched high and low, and dragged the river for his body, but in vain.

Early the third morning Tom Sawyer went poking among some old empty hogsheads down behind the old abandoned house, and in one of them he found the runaway. Huck had just breakfasted upon some stolen odds and ends of food, and was lying down comfortably. He was unkempt, uncombed, and clad in the same old rags that he wore in the days when he was free and happy.

Tom told him the trouble he had been causing, and urged him to go home. Huck's face lost its peaceful look, and took a melancholy shade.

He said, "Don't talk about it, Tom. I've tried it, and it didn't work. It isn't for me; I am not used to it. The Widow's good to me, but I can't stand her ways. She makes me get up just at the same time every morning; she makes me wash, and comb, she won't let me sleep in the woodshed, I've got to wear those clean and starched clothes that just smother me, and I got to go to church and sweat and sweat. I got to wear shoes all Sunday. I have to do everything at a particular hour - everything's so awfully regular that I can't stand it."

"Well, everybody does that way, Huck."

"Tom, it doesn't make any difference. I am not everybody, and I can't stand it."

Tom tried to convince Huck to return in every way he could think of. But nothing worked. Huck was adamant. Finally, Tom hit upon an idea.

"But Huck, we can't let you into the gang if you aren't respectable, you know."

Huck was at once full of concern.

"Can't let me in, Tom? But you let me join you as a pirate?"

"Yes, but that's different. A robber is much more high-toned than a gang of pirates."

"Now, Tom, haven't you always been my friend? You wouldn't leave me out, would you?" pleaded Huck.

"Huck, I don't want to - but what would people say? Why, they'd say, 'Huh! Tom Sawyer's Gang has pretty low characters in it!' And they'd mean you, Huck. You wouldn't like that, and I wouldn't."

Huck was silent for some time, engaged in a mental struggle. Finally he said, "Well, I'll go back to the Widow for a month and see if I can stand it, if you'll let me join the gang, Tom."

"All right, Huck, it's a deal! Come along, old chap."

And the two friends walked away together discussing their band of robbers, when and how the band was to be formed, who were to be the members, what rules the members would have to follow, and so on.

"And you've got to swear on a coffin, and sign it with blood," Tom concluded his recital of the initiating ceremony of the gang of robbers.

"Now, that's something I like!" cheered Huck. "Why, it's a million times more fantastic than pirating. I'll now stay with the Widow till I rot, Tom; and if I get to be a really great robber, and everybody starts talking about me, I think she'll be proud that she adopted me."

THE END